# A RED BIKINI
# 𝒟REAM

Max Martínez

Arte Público Press
Houston
Texas
1990

This book is made possible by a grant from the National Endowment for the Arts, a federal agency.

Arte Público Press
University of Houston
Houston, Texas 77204-2090

Martínez, Max, 1943–
   A Red Bikini Dream / Max Martínez.
      p. cm.
   ISBN 1-55885-001-5
   I. Title.
PS3563.A73344R44 1990                    89-35416
813'.54–dc20                                   CIP

**Photo by Evangelina Vigil-Piñón**

The paper used in this publication meets the minimum requirements of the American National Standard for Permanence of Paper for Printed Library Materials Z39.48-1984. ∞

Books by Max Martínez

*The Adventures of the Chicano Kid*

*Schoolland*

*A Red Bikini Dream*

For Karin

# Contents

A Red Bikini Dream      11

Rancho Notorious      40

The Little Tin Sailor      73

A Sandwich at Blimpy's      98

Bink's Waltz      123

# A Red Bikini Dream

# A Red Bikini Dream

The dream always begins each time in the same way. It is mid-morning. A muggy day, hot, humid. In the distance loom the Berkshires, green and dark and bulky. The sky is a cloudless powder blue. From the base of the sundeck, a wide stretch of green grass slopes. The patch of green holds its line against the tangled weeds and taunting foliage of the forest. There is something, someone, she doesn't know which, in the penumbra just at the edge of the forest. It, he, waits.

She is doing her ironing, nude except for a pair of red bikini underpants, the thin diaphanous material of which spreads tautly over her rounded buttocks. Her shoulder-length hair is pinned up on top of her head in a loose, precarious pile that allows the rare hushed breezes sweeping down from the mountains to cool and refresh her neck. There are beads of sweat on her forehead, on her arms, and in the valley between her breasts.

As she does her ironing, she is expecting something, someone. She is impatient for it, him, to come into the light. She can feel a presence in the forest. She turns several times to peer beyond the trees, into the shadows. A branch on a tree beside the house sways and creaks. A bush shudders as a small bird darts into the air.

She resumes her ironing with a shrug of her shoulders. A tremor shoots through her body. In the rapid movement, her hair comes loose, cascading to rest upon her shoulders. It won't be long. The presence in the forest is in motion. She can feel it, him. A cold flush begins at the back of her legs, moves up through the vulnerable flesh of her inner thighs, courses upward to concentrate itself between her shoulder blades at the base of her neck. Her hair feels stiff and heavy, burdensome and nagging.

Something, someone, is coming now. She is afraid, expectant, impatient, filled with longing, desire. Her arms itch under the skin. A riptide of anticipation swells in her throat. She is eager. She wants to turn and look, to face who it is. She knows what he has come for. She will not turn. Her lips part, glazed with saliva, trembling. She knows it is a man from the way he disturbs the air around her. She has been waiting for him for a long time. She sets the iron to rest on a metal disc. She wants to let him know she is glad he has come, that she is ready for him, that she wants him. She wants to signal that she will not resist, that her submission is complete, total. Her words congeal, she turns to stone.

She can sense him lifting his right foot, dark, brown, with a calloused underside; she feels the steps to the sundeck bend under the pressure of his weight. He is on the sundeck, moving lithely, gently like a zephyr, until he is so close to her that she can feel his breath, warm and moist on her back. It feels like the hushed breezes that sweep down from the mountains. His hands brush her shoulders and glide down her upper arms.

Suddenly the full-length of his naked body is touching hers. His hands descend to her forearms, wrists, caress her slender fingers, stopping to explore and gently press each fingertip, fingertip by fingertip.

His hands drop, as though he has carelessly tossed them away. They come to rest on her tanned, muscular thighs. He presses closer to her, the curve of her back perfectly congruent with the swell of his chest and belly. His hands follow the round shape of her thighs and meet and begin an upward sweep to where the red bikini underpants start to flare in opposite directions, up and over her hips. His touch ignites each nerve in the soft flesh at the sides of her belly. He traces the curve of each rib and he stops, finally, under her arms.

His hands move forward cleaving to the line where the skin of her breasts becomes soft and loose. Each thumb brushes lightly along the parabola of her breasts. Cat-like, he lands upon her nipples, perches voluptuously until they become distended, hard, erupting with life. A long, slow, guttural moan surges upward and escapes as a whimper through her parted lips as she shudders, shakes, and struggles to maintain control. He draws her body against his fluid, forceful, entreating sinew. He pinions her forearms. His face is in her hair, lost in its tangles and shadows, searching for her, creeping toward her.

The man's hands move downward, away from the twin beacons of her nipples. He laces his fingers as his hands meet on the soft plain of her belly, a belly barren and fallow. She can feel the pressure build just above her pelvis. She tenses as he slides in and hooks his thumbs on the elastic waistband of her red bikini underpants. In one long slow movement his hands go lower, dragging the thin material over the round mounds of her buttocks. The red bikini underpants become stuck, resist, at the juncture of her legs where the plump flesh of her inner thighs is pressed together. The elastic cloth begins to stretch as he lowers them over the smooth skin of her eggshell brown thighs. She shifts her weight to one leg and then quickly shifts it to the other. The red bikini underpants snap loose and become bunched in a wrinkled lump between her lower thighs.

He has broken through the tangled veil of her hair. She feels the stubble of his beard on her shoulder blade, rasping along the ridge of her spine, down to the pockmark at her tailbone, over the swell of her buttocks. He stoops to roll the red bikini underpants over her knees, down her bulky calves, and then they drop of their own weight down into a vanquished pile around her ankles.

She lifts one leg up to pull them over the heel. With her free foot she pins them to the sundeck while she pulls them off her other foot. Meanwhile, the stubbled cheek rasps against her neck once more, nudging her earlobes. His hands swoop and flutter in front of her. Her nipples jut forward to meet the talons of his fingers. They squeeze, mash, press, lift, balance, hold and knead her breasts. Another shudder and she leans all the way to press her back against his hairy chest. Her mouth is agape, her eyes are closed, her hands balled into dampened fists.

His erect penis slithers, snake-like and inquisitive, cold and hard and flat into the crevice of her buttocks. He rocks her to and fro. There is an icy chill, goosebumps, radiating over the round plump flesh of her buttocks. His hands on her hips push her body away from his. The cold, erect, penis meanders over the hump of her buttocks. She can feel the engorged, pulsating veins of his penis, serpents in relief upon the snake.

The ironing board tilts over, teetering precariously for an instant before it crashes down on the sundeck. The iron and the metal disc topple along with it. She, too, has gone over, tilting forward, but the man restrains her and draws her back to him. In the brief separation of their bodies, the man's stiff cold organ slides over her swelling buttocks, never losing touch of her. As he draws her back to him, the penis snuggles, chill and wet against the puckered button of her anus.

She is desperate to touch, to feel, to consume, his flesh as she explores him with the palms of her hands. She reaches behind to anchor herself on his muscular thighs. As she gains purchase, he touches her elbows, forces them forward. His hands are on the flat of her back bending her over until she can see her distorted face on the stainless steel metal disc where the iron rested. His bare foot taps one ankle bone, then the other, and she parts her legs as far apart as they can go.

The flat of his hand, fingers spread apart, bridges the mounds of her behind and slides down, fingers coming together as they reach into the thatch of her pubic hair. There, in the moist tangle of wiry hair, he spreads her flesh apart, a pale, pink, milky grotto. She can smell her own musk. He pulls her to him.

She has her hands on her knees, her hair dangling sweetly over the sides of her face. She is waiting, expectant, longing, eager. She feels his ice-cold member, rigid and unyielding, shove into the gaping mouth of her parted flesh. She waits for the warm moist receptacle of her body to overcome the unrelenting ice cold of his penis. He goes no further than the insertion inside the threshold. She waits and he waits. She can feel no other part of him. If he had a body, she can no longer be sure, it is gone, irrelevant, superfluous. All she can feel is the cold, steely feel of the organ, poised for further intrusion.

The shaft of cold begins to move up into the liquid passage of her body. It is a long slow insertion that seems to never end, that spreads out ice cold tentacles whose suction draws forth sensations she has never before experienced. The cold slithering insertion continues, ballooning inside her body. She has reached the limits of her capacity. Her skin, every bit of her skin, is stretched, tingling at the point of imminent rupture.

If she could, she would beg for surcease, a pause in the insertion while her body accepts the intrusion of the ice cold organ, while it becomes a part of her and she a part of it. If she could. She is past rational thought. She is past the point where she can heed the admonitions of her body, the unthought thoughts of care and prevention and caution, the knowledge primeval that there is danger beyond the body's limit.

She orgasms. At the instant of her orgasm, the shaft of cold loses its material presence to become immanent. There is not a cell in her body insensitive to her orgasmic release. A joyous, wondrous, conjunction of biological expression, singing, in clear and precious tones, the song of itself. At this moment, in this place, the universe is present, in a cell, in her body, in the forest, the mountains, in the sky. She has but to touch herself for the rippling throes of orgasm to begin again.

The steady hissing of the car's air conditioner lulled Carrie Rasmussen into a floating, dream-like trance. The road was West Texas flat, two hundred miles beyond San Antonio, with nary a tree, nary a hill in sight. Not a town to break the monotony of the endless miles. For all the terrain varied, she might have been standing still. The instrument panel of the rental car indicated the speed at which she moved, the miles she had travelled, the fuel consumed. For nearly an hour, she had not met any cars coming toward her and neither had she seen a car in the rear view mirror. She used the edges of her consciousness to keep the car in the proper lane, staying within her allocated space through the opaque prism of her trance.

Carrie had been driving since six in the morning. She spent the night in a high rise hotel on the outskirts of San Antonio, adjacent to Interstate 10. At dawn she was awakened by a perfunctory call, as she had instructed. Through the plate-glass window, she saw streaks of orange and yellow splashed delicately over the horizon. She had wondered if it were daylight in Boston. While she waited for the parking lot valet to bring round the car, she felt the thick, oppressive, wet air of morning. Within minutes she had bypassed the headlights of pre-rush hour traffic and was enjoying the Hill Country at sunrise. By noon, after a breakfast of egg and muffin at a fast food restaurant and several stops for coffee, she'd gone through Junction. Past Fort Stockton, she drove along a route that was sere and indifferent, inhospitable and forbidding.

It was nearing two o'clock in the afternoon. The sun was directly overhead, so hot that it blistered the roof of the car, straining the air conditioner. Carrie thought it might be time to stop and rest, wait for the cool of the evening before pushing on. Her joints were stiff, her eyes felt like tiny pinpoints inside a wad of cotton. A dull ache of hunger settled into the pit of her stomach. She wanted a brisk, pelting shower, a nap, and some food.

If she could rest and be on the road again by six or seven in the evening, she could easily make Las Vegas by dawn. She had planned the trip carefully, methodically, in the plodding way she had, leaving no detail to chance. She had allowed for an occasional excursus, to take a scenic route, a detour to see things she might never again have the opportunity to see. Thus far the trip had been direct, without a moment lost to whimsy. Even though she might plan for it, it was not in her nature to give in to it.

Her cigarettes were on the plush velour passenger seat on top of the road map. She lit one and picked up the map. It was a trip booklet prepared by an auto club in Boston. As she studied the map, she darted glances to the road out of a corner of her eye. With tentative eyes, she traced the road she had travelled since six o'clock in the morning, following the green magic marker arrows to locate her present position. Seven full hours of driving. She calculated a rough estimate of ten miles to the next town. It would have to do. She tossed the map aside and fixed her eyes on the road again. In a matter of minutes, the town appeared as a shimmering mirage in a basin surrounded by low-slung hills. Once she was on flat ground, the hills seemed to hide themselves in the purple distance.

Flat, one-story buildings flanked the blacktop gash that cut through the town. The older, wooden ones had the false-fronts of the Old West. White, ash-like sand partially covered over the asphalt as the desert tried to reclaim the part of itself that lay beneath the trespass of civilization. Before she entered the town proper, Carrie had scanned both strips of buildings for a place to stay. She noticed the hotel immediately but was put off by the false front that leaned to one side as if the roof had partly caved in. Nevertheless, assuming that she had no other choice, she turned into one of the angled parking lanes. She kept the motor running as she looked the hotel over.

The large picture windows on either side of the entrance to the hotel appeared to have a film of grime at least a century old. There was a half-moon scar, curving from top to bottom on one of the windows. Carrie became discouraged and apprehensive at the alternative of driving further on before finding a clean enough, decent place to rest. She turned her head away from the hotel, toward the western end of town. Her spirits lifted a little when she saw the sign that announced a motel. She threw the car in reverse and headed in the direction of the motel. She crossed her fingers for luck.


Carrie Rasmussen sped through town in a few seconds. The motel was built at an angle to the main street, removed from the cluster of town buildings, seated upon a mound of sandy soil, solitary and diffident. Behind the motel, the crisply clean blacktop with its bold yellow center strip beckoned to El Paso.

She turned into the motel driveway, stopping on the concrete floor of a carport. In front of her, in the thick plate glass window Carrie could see the full extension of the main street in reflection, with its gray sunbleached ribbon of asphalt. The heat rising from the powdery white sand shimmered in the reflection.

Carrie opened the door to admit a gust of searing heat into the air conditioned interior of the car. She had been breathing treated air for hours. The furnace blast of desert heat blistered her arms, neck and cheeks. She shivered slightly at the sudden change in climate, becoming acclimated to it in a matter of seconds, and then she found it unbearable not more than a few seconds after that.

Inside the motel lobby, the heat was as unbearable as it was outside, with the added irritation of a musty, stiffling smell. A young girl, about seventeen, lay on a beach towel next to a rickety coffee table in the narrow reception area. She lay on her stomach, wore jeans and a swimsuit top which was untied in back. A pancake-size rim of breast squeezed out from her ribcage. Her forearms were stacked on top of each other, her head resting on them. When the girl heard the door open, she lifted her head to get a good look at Carrie Rasmussen.

"Hello. Do you want a room," the girl asked, desultorily.

Carrie did not immediately respond. She remained just inside the door, clutching her purse at waist level. The hours of driving, the road fatigue, made it difficult for her to speak. She removed her sunglasses, tilted her head and ran her fingers through her hair.

The girl lifted up on her arms as if she were going to do a push-up, and in a quick motion swung around to a sitting position, her legs crossed Indian-fashion. The loose swimsuit top bunched between her breasts with their plum-sized nipples pointing in opposite directions. Her jeans were unbuttoned at the waist. The girl had massive breasts that drooped flabbily down to her thin waist. She was not in the least embarrassed that Carrie watched her as she tucked each breast into the swimsuit top which was much too small for the formidable task expected of it. The girl leaned forward to tie the straps into a bow in back.

The girl wobbled unsteadily as she got to her feet.

"Check-in card's right on the counter, ma'am," the girl said. Her bleached blond hair fell thick and smooth along the sides of her face. "You fill it out. I have to go potty. I'll be right back. Okay?"

As she walked away, Carrie noticed the girl's buttocks disproportionately large and heart-shaped. She would be a very fat girl were it not for the thin waist.

The mephitis of the lobby reminded her of putrescent diapers. Her forehead began to perspire, her forearms felt clammy. Carrie filled in her name on the card, her home address in Boston, and left the space blank that asked how long she intended to stay.

The young girl came back with her hair brushed and pinned with two pink butterfly barrettes. There was a reddish glow on her cheeks, forehead and nose from the scrubbing she'd given her face. She'd put on a blue gingham western-cut shirt, that had mother-of-pearl buttons. She had not bothered to tuck the shirt into her jeans.

Carrie Rasmussen pushed the check-in card toward the young clerk. She'd taken out her clutchpurse which lay on the counter between her hands.

"How long are you going to stay," asked the young girl.

"Just long enough for a shower and a quick nap," answered Carrie.

"Yeah, I thought so. We get lots like that, here," the girl said. "Overnights is mostly what we get. Truckers'll come in, sometimes, you know, take a bath, sleep a little. Then they hassle with us. They think they shouldn't have to pay for a full day if they're here for just a few hours. They just took a bath, they think. What's a bath? It ain't worth twenty-seven fifty. They think."

The girl made some notations on the bottom of the check-in slip. Her tongue spilled over her lower lip as she concentrated on separating the two pieces.

"Cash or charge?" she asked.

Carrie took a charge card from one of the plastic pockets of her clutchpurse. It was the card she had designated for travel expenses.

The girl's massive breasts swayed ponderously when she slid the embosser grip back and forth over Carrie's credit card. The girl stapled the charge slip to the check-in card and slipped them into a drawer in the cash register. She handed Carrie her charge card.

"You sign the charge ticket when you check out," the girl explained.

"I can sign the charge now," said Carrie.

"Sorry," the girl said, "My daddy's rules. You have to sign it when you check-out. Just drive your car straight ahead from where you are and you'll come to the room. The air conditioner works pretty good in that room. About half of them, the units, are broke; including the one in here, darn it! Daddy says if we can stick it out the rest of this year, you know, we'll be able to move out to California. I can't wait. I'd sure like to go surfing."

The young girl smiled generously and clasped her hands in front of her, hunching her shoulders. Carrie returned a thin smile before going outside to the car.


From the trunk of the car, she retrieved a medium-sized suitcase in which she had packed clothes for the journey and a make-up kit. Inside her room, the air was thick and mildewed, trapped and unmoved for what seemed to be months. A shaft of sun light pierced the center of the room. Dust motes lingered in mid-air. In the brief minutes that she had surrendered the car's air conditioner, Carrie Rasmussen had perspired heavily. There was a sizable sweat stain, which she deplored, on her blouse. She felt her underthings clinging and clammy, uncomfortable on her damp skin.

Carrie placed her bags near a dresser, beside a scuffed chair. She sighed deeply and lay fully clothed on top of one of the two beds in the room. The bedspread was cheap and rough. She sighed in disgust, closed her eyes to keep from looking at the rust-colored water stains on the ceiling. After a little while, sighing deeply again, she sat up to undo the straps of her sandals. While she sat up, she removed her blouse, which she examined, frowned, and tossed on the floor beside the bags. She unhooked her brassiere but did not remove it. She unbuttoned her trousers and pulled down the side zipper. She took several deep breaths, and then she bent forward. Doubled over, she pushed her hair over her head to allow the back of her neck to breathe.

The air conditioner was a wall unit stuck high into the wall as close to the ceiling as possible. A number of the plastic slats were missing from the filter cover. Carrie walked under it, stood on tiptoe to flip the on-switch, but nothing happened. The thick power cord dangled beside the outlet. She cursed softly and stooped to plug it in. Instantly the air conditioner began to roar. In a few more seconds, it settled into its operating speed, alternately rattling and purring in a gentle roar.

She came back to the side of the bed where she began to remove her trousers. When they were bunched at her ankles, she pulled one foot and then the other, after which she kicked them toward the suitcases. She removed her brassiere and tossed it after the trousers. She pulled at the red bikini underpants to let some air in. The noise of the air conditioner became less annoyingly insistent, as if wearing itself out, settling to a soft, almost reassuring purr. Carrie Rasmussen closed her eyes and lay on the bed to rest a few minutes before her shower.


After lying in bed for nearly fifteen minutes, the room still had not cooled. She tossed and turned, shifted her body belly up to belly down, without finding a position comfortable enough to keep still. The feeling of anxiousness would not subside. She convinced herself that she was tired from driving all day. There was more to it, but Carrie had resolved not to think about it. She needed a hot bath, a good solid hour of soaking in warm water.

She got up from the bed, walked to the dresser where she'd placed her purse and cigarettes. She lit one and looked at herself in the dresser mirror. She stepped back to get a good look at herself. The image was too close, the perspective all wrong. She stepped back further until she touched the foot of the bed. She cradled an elbow in her right hand, the cigarette inserted between two fingers, inches from her mouth. She felt the claustrophobia of the room drawing in on her.

Carrie Rasmussen had reached an ageless maturity in her mid-twenties which, aided by a carefully annotated carriage, would last her for at least another decade. Her shoulders were too wide, boney; her breasts were a mite too small, but still round, softer perhaps than she would prefer. They had developed rapidly while she was a teenager and had remained unchanged ever since. The rest of her body, from her waist down, was well-rounded and firm. There was just a slight forward swell of her belly which no amount of exercise had been able to flatten.

Carrie didn't want to watch herself. She turned, paced between the beds toward the wall, flicking on the bedlamp before retracing her steps. A brief, inadvertent glimpse into the mirror revealed her image with the light behind her. She appeared as a blur, the sharp outlines of her body effaced, ghostly, indistinct from the furniture in the room. Only the red bikini underpants stood out. Back at the dresser, she picked up the ashtray to carry with her and began to pace. After fifteen years, she'd started to smoke again. When she felt the heat of the cigarette ember on her fingers, she stubbed it out impatiently. She tossed the ashtray back on the dresser, purposely avoiding the image of herself in the mirror.


Carrie placed the suitcase on top of the chair and the make-up kit atop the dresser. The pack of cigarettes was empty. She wadded it up to toss in the wastebasket and remembered that she'd opened it the night before, right after dinner. She was smoking too much. She threw open the suitcase and took another pack from the carton that lay diagonally over the neatly folded clothes. She opened the fresh pack of cigarettes, withdrew one, but did not light it. Instead, leaving the cigarette dangling from her parted lips, she took out a change of clothing.

The air conditioner still had not dissolved the sultry oppressiveness of the room.

Carrie removed her underwear, wadding it up, feeling it warm and damp. She plucked from the suitcase a white plastic garbage bag in which she stored her dirty clothes. She dropped in her panties, picked up the remainder of her clothing from the floor. She debated whether she might stand to wear the trousers again, decided no, and stuffed them into the bag as well. The cigarette in her mouth was wet. She pulled it from her mouth, frowned, broke it in half, tossed it in the waste basket. She picked up the pack of cigarettes, along with her lighter. She'd have a leisurely smoke in the tub.

As she headed for the bathroom, she stopped suddenly, turned, a flush of apprehension piercing through her body. It was the presence of the unseen man who came to her in dreams. She heard the whirr of the air conditioner behind her, saw the shabbiness of the room. She had felt someone in the room, she was sure of it. Carrie leaned against the door jamb, pressed the back of her head against the wood, closed her eyes. She waited. Her blood began to race, her heart beat faster, there was a tingle in her fingertips, goose bumps streaked along her arms and thighs. Just as suddenly as she felt it, the presence disappeared. Everything became still and quiet in the room, the palpable silence broken only by the sputtering whirr of the air conditioner. She wanted to draw the dream into her waking life.

Knowing it was not to be, Carrie placed a bag containing toilet articles, cigarettes and lighter on top of the toilet tank. She stooped over to open the hot water tap of the tub. While she waited, as was her habit before stepping into the bathtub, she first brushed her teeth, keeping her face close to the running water. The water was hot but not steaming, as she liked it. The mechanism to stop the tub from draining did not work. She compressed her lips to express her dissatisfaction, tried the shower and was relieved when the water began to gush overhead.

Under the shower tap, she stood still, feet slightly apart, letting the jet of water pelt her back. She closed her eyes tightly until she no longer felt the pinpricks of the water. She saw herself standing before an ironing board wearing a pair of red bikini underpants. The image was sharp and clear before her. She felt her nipples become erect and she crossed her hands over her breasts. She drew her shoulders forward, dropped her chin against her chest. She squeezed her breasts until she felt pain. Nothing happened. Slowly, she lowered her hands, uncrossing them, drawing them apart, lowering them further, then recrossing them one on top of the other, pressing in the soft flesh of her lower belly. She lowered them still further, on the crest of her Mound of Venus, into the thick thatch of pubic hair. Nothing happened.

She finished her shower quickly, briskly toweled herself dry, wrapped herself in the damp towel, tucking it high up under her arms. When she came out of the bathroom, the air in the room had cooled considerably. Along with the change in temperature, she could smell the stronger stench of the stale air circulating. The initial nausea gave way to the feeling of claustrophobia.

She felt penned in, swept up by an overpowering urge to leave the room, to get out in the open. She took several deep breaths before she set the suitcase on the floor and sat in the chair facing the mirror on the dresser. The anxiety went away and she relaxed a little. She lit a cigarette. The ends of her wet hair, resting on her shoulders, felt cold and alien.

Carrie leaned closer to the mirror for a better look at her face. The reflection of her face revealed a line or two that she was certain had not been there when she left Boston. She was tired from the trip and from the strain of her disintegrating life. She consoled herself in the knowledge that she would get used to things eventually. Maybe then, she told herself, the lines will go away.

Thus reassured, she settled back in the chair. She leaned over to retrieve a hairbrush with a silver handle from the suitcase. She began to brush her wet hair. After each pass, she snapped it in the air to shake away the accumulated water. As if a sudden thought had occurred to her, she stopped and began to tap the handle of the silver hairbrush rhythmically on the formica top of the dresser. She lowered her eyes, exhaled noisily, became pensive. She abruptly tossed the brush away. It fell with a jarring clatter. She drew deeply from her cigarette, held her breath, mashed the butt forcefully into the ashtray.

The muscles on either side of her mouth tightened into sharply defined dimples. She pulled on the ends of the towel and let it fall into a pile around her waist. She brushed the towel off of her thighs. She stared directly into the mirror with a look that was defiant, unapologetic. She pressed her hands, fingers fanned out, flat against each breast. Pressing forcefully, she shoved her hands toward each other and then she separated her thumb and forefinger to allow her nipples to burst forth. She squeezed each nipple until it swelled, became purplish-black and hard. She inclined her head, puckered her lips and blew soft, warm air to one and then the other.

She let go of her breasts abruptly and began to scratch the upper line of her damp pubic hair. Slowly she dragged the silver hairbrush along the dresser top and dropped it into her lap. The bristle side dug into her thighs. Carrie jammed the handle of it between her legs and squeezed her thighs tightly. She raised her leg, drew it over the other and leaned back against the chair, her weight resting on one buttock.

Careful to avoid her reflection in the mirror, she got up to move to the bed. Before doing so, she took a pair of red bikini panties from the suitcase and hurriedly put them on. She stripped the bed of its covers and lay down in the center of it. The sheet underneath was stiff and warm, a pleasant contrast to the cool air now circulating in the room. She stretched out her arms perpendicular to her sides. Her hands, in one of which she held the hairbrush, overlapped the edge of the bed.

She touched the tip of the hairbrush handle to her right breast, gently, without pressure. She brought her left hand between her legs, applied a little pressure, and held it there. She closed her eyes lightly and began to imagine the Berkshire zephyrs delicately brushing over her body. The image was so vivid she could feel the two by fours of the sundeck under her bare feet. There was a warm glow on her shoulders from the sun. She was completely relaxed, feeling a persistent tingling between her thighs.

Carrie lay the silver hairbrush on her belly and began to brush the tips of her fingers over her breasts, tracing over the contours, drawing geometric shapes. She closed her eyes tightly and before too long, fleetingly, she sensed the presence of the naked man in the darkness of the forest, moving on bare feet toward her. She could see his feet moving, his hands swinging at his side. She'd dreamt it so many times, she knew its rhythms and movements, and its turns. The beginning of it, its overtures of desire and longing, of anticipation and mounting sexual intensity, these she could duplicate.

It was never the same as the dream, though. However perfectly she could recreate the dream, her consciousness was superimposed over it, willing it to happen. She could linger for long moments on those sensations in the dream that brought her the most intense pleasure. Sud-

denly, much too soon, she would become conscious that she was manip-
ulating herself, that she was not dreaming at all. In the end, she could
never recreate the dream nor its effects. No amount of self-stimulation
brought the feeling of completeness that she felt upon waking.


She pulled on her nipples, twirling them and then pressing down on
them, as in her fantasy she sensed the man coming closer to the edge
of the forest. She pressed her eyes down tightly as if the effort itself
would draw the naked man out of the dark and on to her waiting body.
She put her knees together and sallied her hips on the bed. She had
a sense, palpable and urgent, that the man was watching her, taking in
each thing she did, but that he would not come forward, that he chose
in fact to remain at the edge of the forest, in the dark, watching. In the
things she did to herself, under his watchful eye, she did for him. She
sought his approval, imagined his arousal, stiff and angled up from his
belly.

Her nerves, her energy, her entire existence began to concentrate in
the region of her pubic hair. Beneath the thick and curly sprout, pressed
in by her bikini underpants, she felt the loose flesh at the entrance to her
vagina become wet, puffed, and throbbing. The imagined man became a
vague idea, losing shape and vitality, fading. He became effaced beyond
her ability to draw his tactile presence to the moment she created. She
grabbed the hairbrush and gently tapped her pelvic bone. A flush, as if
released by the tapping, spread through her body, making her aware of
how cold the room had become.

She let go of the hairbrush, leaving it on the flat of her lower belly,
feeling the pressure of its weight. She strained with all her might, arched
the small of her back, compressed her sphincter, lifted her hips, drew
her lips tightly over her teeth. Carrie tensed suddenly, as if a jolt of
electricity had passed through her body. She shot her legs forward,
pointing her toes so they became parallel to the bed. A great wondrous
tremor, erupting from the chasm of unfulfilled yearning, rumbled over
the planes and contours of her body, rolling in wave after wave. Her
entire body became covered in a film of perspiration.

Carrie felt herself levitate, suspended from the pull of the earth-
bound life she led. Tense, taut, like a wire pulled between two points,
there was the hum of atoms in chaos, pulling willy nilly to restore their
deviated orbits.

She rolled the red bikini underpants midway down her thighs after
which she grabbed the silver brush by the square bed of its bristles and
applied the handle of it to her mound of Venus. A long, low groaning
moan began deep in her chest. The sound of it came up as a whimper,

cat-like and tenuous, like a fire engine siren drawing near. She took the hairbrush in both of her hands, pressing the flat of it against the swelling she felt in her belly. She felt the bristles prick her palm as she slid the brush further down. She turned it a little, aiming the handle forward and over her mound of Venus. She slid the silvertip along the viscous parting of her body.

When she felt it coming, she hunched her shoulders together, threw her arms wide, gripped the sides of the bed. She popped suddenly. She expelled a series of gasps that carried abrupt, jerking moans along with them. These were followed by short, brief tremors that she was unable to control. She raised her legs a little, the brush pinioned by the taut muscles of her thighs.

She was able to summon forth the pleasurable sensations for several more minutes before they stopped altogether and she collapsed, exhausted, breathing heavily, enjoying the feel of clean perspiration over her body. Carrie curled up her legs, rolled over on her side, keeping her hands clasped between her legs. Her mouth was open, dry. Gradually her eyelids were too heavy to hold up. They were leadlike, turning the hazy sunlit room into complete darkness. In a few seconds, following a series of pained whimpers, she was soundly asleep.

Carrie awoke several hours later, cold and sore from having slept without shifting position. The air conditioner hummed steadily. The room felt like an icebox. She had slept uncovered. Her cheeks and her neck felt swollen, numb. She rolled her legs over the side of the bed, placing her elbows on her knees, holding her head in her hands. Carrie felt stiff and sluggish as she waited for her head to clear. She finally managed to get up on her feet and, in the movement of a sleepwalker, she raised up her underpants. She was able to walk, if a bit wobbly, to the bathroom where she splashed water on her face. She brushed her teeth quickly. When she came out of the bathroom, the chill in the room felt good, especially against her damp face. She curled strands of wet hair over her ears.

She felt sapped and listless. Her face in the mirror was numb and deeply lined with sleep. Her eyes bulged in a pink film with a latticework of red veins. She wanted to sleep more, a lot more. The skin of her body felt clammy. She returned to the bed, covering herself snugly, curling up. She struggled against the sleep that was already settling in over her. She had not planned for this at all. She made one last effort to rise, but the movements were in her mind, as if she were at some distance, observing. In a matter of seconds, Carrie Rasmussen was sound asleep again. When she next awoke, it was dark outside. She dressed quickly and went out to eat.


Sand Jack's had a brightly-lit neon sign that blinked on and off in front. From where she stood in the driveway to the motel, she could see a naked light bulb stuck over the entrance. To the left side of the entrance, there was a dirt-encrusted picture window. About a half dozen vehicles, mostly pick-up trucks, were parked in the gravel lot. There was no need for the car. She began to cross the road, finding the absence of any traffic disconcerting. She walked over cautiously nevertheless feeling in her bones the premonition of a speeding truck bearing down on her, that it would come upon her so suddenly that she'd be unable to get out of the way in time.

The voices of Dwight Yoakum and Buck Owens on the jukebox, singing, "The Streets of Bakersfield" met her as she opened the door. To her left was a small eating area, four tables, on which reposed napkin dispensers, salt and pepper shakers, plastic-covered menus, bottles of ketchup and hot sauce, ashtrays. Carrie selected one of the tables. She brought out her cigarettes and lighter, lit one, and placed the package, lighter over it, in front of the napkin dispenser.

On the other side of Sand Jack's were more tables where men in hats and cowboy clothes sat. There was a small U-shaped bar to separate the two areas. No one sat at the bar. At the far end of the room was the jukebox, blaring a hard rock and roll number by Hank Williams, Jr, "If you don't like Hank Williams, you can kiss our ass!" The men concentrated their attention on a game of pool.

She waited a long time before a waitress, who had been inside the kitchen area, came to her. The waitress carried a gallon can of ketchup under one arm and a funnel in her hand.

"Hello, dearie," said the waitress, "where did you come from?"

"Are you closing," asked Carrie.

"Just about," the waitress said. "We were just putting up everything. If you're hungry, we won't turn you away. Can't make no money turning away hungry people, I always say. I'm sure the cook'll rustle up something for you."

Carrie bit her fingernail as she began to read the menu. Nothing seemed to quite stir her appetite. The elderly waitress recognized Carrie's reluctance to settle on anything and recommended a chopped sirloin steak because it was just about all they had left that was either fresh or out of the freezer. Carrie gave her assent, grateful that the choice was taken away from her. She asked for a beer while she waited. The waitress brought her beer right away. It was wrapped in sandwich paper. She placed it alongside a small glass and slid the salt shaker beside them.

"I'll be right out with your salad," she said, and waddled away through the swinging door into the kitchen.

Carrie had no sooner finished the salad, coated with a vinegary thousand island dressing, than the waitress came out again, gliding gracefully for so large a woman with a plate held over her head. The steak turned out to be an oversized, overcooked hamburger, drowned in a gravy that was thick and lumpy, streaked with blackened pan drippings and black flecks of pepper. It was capped with a mound of translucent, mushy onions. Next to it was a pile of thick french-fried potatoes, broad and bulky like railroad ties. Carrie pushed aside as much of the gravy as was possible and all of the onions. The coating of gravy remaining on the meat was more like a salty film. On a green plastic basket were four diagonally-sliced pieces of Texas toast. She liked the Texas toast, as she had never seen a slice of bread quite so thick.

The salty, pungent taste of the sirloin was attenuated by the odd aftertaste of the beer. She found that if she followed each bite with a sip of beer, the food went down without making her gag. Still, Carrie was hungry, which made things easier. She ate and drank quickly since there was no one to talk to. She felt rushed, wanting to hurry, even though she had decided not to push on after all. She would wait until morning to get going.

The waitress came back, toweling her arms dry. Strands of hair had escaped their pinning and were plastered on her forehead. She was short of breath.

"Did you want another beer, honey?" she asked.

Carrie said, "Yes, please," on impulse.

The Mexican wore jeans and a black t-shirt under his denim jacket. The black gimme cap on his head carried a Jack Daniel's advertisement. His pectoral muscles were pronounced, effeminate, under the t-shirt. Upon entering Sand Jack's, he walked immediately to the right, past the empty bar, where he made the rounds, shaking hands, stopping briefly to converse with each man present. When he had finished, he took a stool at the bar, spreading out his arms over it. He kibitzed good-naturedly with the pool players, who were in no mood to talk to anyone. He walked over to the eating area, where he took a table next Carrie.

He appeared to be thirty, although given his Indian features, he might have been five years younger or older. His lips were full and fleshy. As he sat down, an incipient beer belly insinuated itself over his lap. The waitress had seen him enter and without his having to order, brought him a plate similar to the one she had brought to Carrie.

"You want a beer with that," the waitress asked.

"Does a bear shit on a sand dune," he said, already beginning to pour salt and ketchup on the french fries.

"There ain't any bears around here, and you know it," said the waitress.

He caught Carrie observing him and tipped the gimme cap to her. He grinned and winked, as if to say he was kidding with the waitress. Carrie turned her head away quickly, embarrassed to have been caught staring. She poured the last of the beer bottle in the glass.

"Could you stand to have another beer, if I bought you one," the Mexican asked Carrie Rasmussen.

Carrie assented, surprised at herself for doing so. The waitress frowned when the Mexican sent her back for another beer. He leaned over.

"Listen, I hate to eat by myself. What say, I join you. Or, you join me." He smiled with large, square teeth, saluting her with the beer bottle before upending it over his open mouth. He did not touch his lips to the bottle as he poured straight into his gullet.

"Why don't I join you," said Carrie. "I'm already finished and you've just begun to eat."

"That's real nice of you. Come on over," he said, pulling out a chair for her.


The Mexican swallowed the morsel he chewed, wiped his hands with a paper napkin, told her his name, and stretched out his hand across the table. Carrie reached out her hand and told him her name.

"Passing through?" he said, pleasantly, cutting the entire sirloin in neat little squares.

"I stopped for some rest this afternoon. I had planned to be on the road after a couple of hours, but I guess I overslept," said Carrie.

The waitress brought Carrie's beer.

"Put that on my bill," said the Mexican.

"Thanks," said Carrie.

"You must be at the motel, 'cross the way," he said.

"Yes, I am," said Carrie, a little uncomfortable.

He speared a square of meat and a tangle of onions into his mouth. A gobbet of gravy dripped onto his chin. He wiped it away before beginning to chew. He look at her intently.

"Reason I mention it, your car's not parked out front," he said.

"I see," she said.

"Truck drivers, truck drivers'll think they can make the stretch be-tween Houston and El Paso, one haul. Takes a lot of amphetamines to do it. They end up here, sack out for the night, sometimes. Interstate's the best thing ever happened to this town. Brought it back to life, I would say."

"What do people do here?" Carrie asked.

"A little of everything. You name it, somebody does it. Ranching. Roughnecking. There's a couple that has a winery. Out there in the desert. How 'bout that? A vineyard out where even the lizards can't make a living."

"I wouldn't expect it. Is it true?" said Carrie.

"Why would I lie?" said the Mexican, and he winked at her, grinning broadly.


Carrie drank her beer, nodded a few times as he made conversation, asked her questions. Otherwise, she kept her part of the conversation to a minimum.

All of a sudden, the thoughts that flashed across her mind caused a nausea to overtake her. The reason she'd accepted his invitation be-came clear to her. The Mexican took it calmly when she gathered her check and picked up her purse.

"I should be going," she said, having a difficult time getting her things together.

"I have a jug of whiskey in my truck," he said, raising an eyebrow to ask the question. His meaning unmistakable, his smile inviting.

"You're married," she said, unsure of herself, softening, indicating the wedding band on his finger.

"So are you," he said, aiming a shake of his head at her ring finger. "That makes us even, doesn't it?"

She had aroused an interest in the Mexican, an interest which was flattering and which went against everything she had known in her life. In the life she left behind her in Boston, men made passes which they knew, expected, would be rebuffed. The Mexican's offer was not flir-tation. It was a proposition, clear and simple, and he waited for her answer.

She was in the middle of the desert, among people she would not see again. She liked the anonymity of the moment, the fact that she did not know this man, the fact that she could ask him to stay afterward, or that she could ask him to go away. It was all up to her.

The decision she made was swift, out of character, irrevocable.

"I'm in room nine," she said, feeling flushed, her adrenalin flowing. "Give me a few minutes."

"You bet," he said, upending the beer bottle, flashing a smile.

The Mexican pushed his unfinished plate of food away and ordered another beer. No one on the other side of Sand Jack's had paid any attention to them. Carrie paid her check and walked out quickly.


At the motel, Carrie undressed quickly, leaving on the pair of red bikini underpants. There was no time for a shower. Instead, she dusted herself liberally with scented powder, rubbing away its white splotches into her pubic hair. She stood in front of the dresser mirror, lit a cigarette, inhaled deeply. She had left the door ajar, decided it wasn't safe, and turned the dead bolt. She waited with her back pressed against it.

The Mexican knocked softly on the door. She could feel the vibrations of his knock on her back. She reached behind to twist the dead bolt. The door creaked discretely when the Mexican pushed it aside. She had walked to the dresser to extinguish the second cigarette.

The Mexican walked in, saw Carrie, her back to him, wearing only her red bikini underpants. He carried a full pint of whiskey. He closed the door behind him and removed his denim jacket, dropping it on the floor. As he walked up to her, he drew the shirttail out of his trousers.

The Mexican drew up close to Carrie. Without preamble, he began to kiss the slope of her neck. His breath reeked of the whiskey. Carrie felt his taut chest through the t-shirt pressed snugly against her back. The rough material of his jeans brushed against the back of her thighs.

"All of it," said Carrie, a tremor in her voice.

"What," said the Mexican.

"Take off all your clothes," said Carrie. "Hurry!"


The Mexican placed the whiskey bottle on the dresser. He began to remove his clothes, as she had ordered. The cigarette she had extinguished flared up again in the ashtray. She mashed it again and picked up the bottle. She drank deeply, feeling the burn of it as it streaked down inside her body, leaving a warm glow in its wake. She dropped her arms to her side.

She heard the Mexican behind her, pulling and jerking on his boots, then on his tight trousers. He came up behind her, bringing both hands round to the swell of her belly. His heaving chest pressed smooth and firm, tight against her shoulder blades. He began a gentle, rocking motion, pivoting on the balls of his feet. His hard penis mashed across her buttocks, his lubricating fluids sopping into the thin material of her panties, becoming a moist spot the size of a quarter. After fondling her liquid breasts for a moment, he put his hands on her shoulders and tried to turn her to face him.

"No, don't," she said, "Don't look at me."

"What the hell is this," he asked, irritated.

"Please," she moaned, "do as I ask."

She took one of his hands and brought it to the waistband of her red bikini underpants. He began to roll them downward, using the flat of his hands, until they took a rope-like shape. He bent down to pull them over her knees, but she stopped him.

"Leave them like that," she said, touching his shoulder.

She spread her legs as far as she could, stretching taut the red material. Then, she bent over.

"Do you want it in the ass," asked the Mexican, misunderstanding her intent. "Is that the way you want it? Up the ass, hunh?"

He took his erect peter and began to make poking, humping motions with it into her anus. He reached down between her legs and ran two fingertips along the crevice of her wet pussy. Carrie shuddered at his touch. The Mexican moved away a little, and began to moisten the puckered button with her own juices. He guided the tip of his dick against her ass and pressed in.

"No, don't," said Carrie in a wounded voice.

"You want it this way, don't you?" said the Mexican, soothingly, cooing, as if trying to coax her into it. "Isn't this the way you want it?"

Carrie twisted sideways to reach around and guide him to the aperture below. Once their bodies were in accord, she placed her hands on her knees and waited as he penetrated the lubricated folds of her flesh and began the slow, on again, off again, measured insertion. He remained immobile, his hands on her hips, rocking her to and fro.

When he had impaled her to the hilt, he began to withdraw, slowly, stopping every second or so, until he came perilously close to slipping out of her entirely. He draped himself over her back, his cheek resting on her spine, as he inched back in, gently, slowly. He repeated the rocking movement several times. Carrie's thigh muscles became taut, coiling. The Mexican kept up a steady, rhythmic, push-me, pull-you; his hands came up from underneath to massage her swaying breasts.

He increased the pace of his thrusts, spreading wide her buttocks to probe deeper, wanting to touch a part of her that seemed beyond reach. He raised himself from her back, pushing her away with the heel of his hands, drawing back with the tips of his fingers hooked over her hips. The Mexican threw his legs apart and pushed up on the balls of his feet. He glanced between their bodies and he placed his hand flat over her tailbone, his thumb going into the cleft between her buttocks, digging inside her anus.

He began a series of jerking grunts, inhaling noisily through his pursed lips. His strokes became shorter, hardly an inch in length, coming in swift, piston-like thrusts. His ramming into her pounded the bones of her butt against his thighs. He shifted the position of his feet on the floor to keep from getting a cramp.

The Mexican groaned long and painfully, and drew her buttocks to him for one last time and he held them against him. She felt the shudders of his orgasm and reached between them to take his balls in her hand. When she touched him, a second orgasmic spasm went through his body and he jerked himself into her some more.

Carrie felt the final involuntary throbbing of his penis inside her body. He was finished. He continued to hold on to her tightly, relaxing a little at a time until his penis shrivelled and the force of gravity yanked it out of her. She remained bent over, her hands on her knees, until she felt the chill of his ejaculate rolling out of her and down her thigh.

Carrie took a step away from the Mexican and drew up the red bikini underpants. He leaned against the dresser, head thrown back, catching his breath. There were beads of perspiration mingled with the hair on his chest. He reached out a hand to her, grinning.

"That was something," he gasped, looking into her eyes for confirmation.

"Get dressed," Carrie snapped.

"This isn't all there is, you know," said the Mexican, shaking his limp dick. "Let's get in bed. This little fucker will be ready to go again in no time."

"I said, get dressed and get out," said Carrie, firmly.

She went into the bathroom, taking her cigarettes, closing the door behind her. She pulled her underpants down around her ankles and sat on the toilet. Her vagina was tender, smeared with her and the Mexican's emissions. She wiped herself carefully, urinated, lit a cigarette. She remained seated on the toilet, elbows on her knees, while she smoked an entire cigarette. Afterward, she kicked away the panties, got into the shower under water as hot as she could stand.

The Mexican was not sure she really wanted him to leave. His vanity told him she couldn't possibly mean it. She'd feel differently once she came out of the bathroom. They had hardly spoken to each other. When he heard the groan of the shower running, he shrugged, gathered up his whiskey and left. He wasn't sure that what he had was a story he would want to tell.

Carrie spent a good twenty minutes in the shower, scrubbing away unsuccessfully at her indiscretion. She felt she had violated a personal code, a standard of decency, which had governed her entire adult life. She had second thoughts about having fucked the man. It was what she had wanted to do, no doubt there, but nevertheless it was a stupid and dangerous thing to do.

She opened the bathroom door an inch or two, apprehensive that he still might be in the room. She breathed a sigh of relief when she saw that the Mexican was gone. The red bikini underpants were on the yellowed floor tiles. She picked them up to stuff them in the plastic bag.

She came out of the bathroom, hair wrapped in a towel. She checked the door and flipped the deadbolt on it. She slipped into the teddy she used to sleep in. She had intended to brush her hair but she felt tired, slightly hung over from the three beers, unable to comply with habits from what seemed to be a long time ago. Carrie turned off all the lights and threw herself on the bed, lying there in the dark, her eyes open.

It had not turned out the way she had expected it would. The Mexican had played his part, perhaps a little too well. He had been sure of movement, swift to complete his pleasure. She was angered by the single-minded method of his fucking. Of course, it wasn't his fault. The terms of the encounter, had they expressed them, made each responsible for the taking of what there was to take.

What she had expected, what she wanted, not the Mexican, and not any other man, could provide. Carrie recalled every movement and sensation of the encounter. His lips on her shoulders, the hair of his chest against her back. None of these bore any resemblance to the dream. His penis, thick and bulky, did not have the clean, cool feel of the male presence in her dreams. The ridiculous, grotesque pounding he'd given her, lost in his own private sport, had little to compare with the even, smooth, entry that she wanted. She had not even had an orgasm. She touched herself, and as quickly as she did, she stopped. There was little point to it, she told herself, and gradually, drifted into a troubled sleep.

At one o'clock in the afternoon, Carrie awoke, groggy and stiff from too much sleep. She was cross with herself because of the time. As she prepared for the day's travel, the Mexican was already becoming a remnant of a past which she did not think she would ever want to resurrect. The sooner she left, the better.

She finished with her make-up, selected a light spaghetti-strap summer dress with a built-in bra for the drive. Thin-strapped sandals completed the outfit. She surveyed the room to make sure she left nothing behind. As she stepped out into the heat of the day, the sun was white-hot, glaring. She put on her dark glasses.

Carrie drove the car to the front desk, leaving the engine and the air conditioner running. She was checked out of the motel by a red-faced man who bore a puffed resemblance to the girl who had checked her in. The man with the drunkard's florid face smiled timidly and told her he appreciated her business.

Carrie drove to the gas station next to Sand Jack's. In fading blue lettering against the whitewash, it advertised groceries, beer, and hunting gear. She stopped beside a pair of rusting pumps. As she stepped down from the car a dust devil came up suddenly and flared her skirt.

She asked the lone attendant inside to fill up the car. While he went outside, she selected some cheese, a plastic tube of braunswiger, and a box of Ritz crackers. Not much of a breakfast, she told herself. Carrie took a cheap styrofoam cooler from a white pyramid in the center of the store. She put it on the counter, went back to the coolers for a six pack of beer, which she dropped in the cooler. The attendant returned and began to total the items on the counter. She asked him to spread a bag of ice over the beer.

She left the town behind her in a matter of seconds. The desert spread itself out before the hood of the car, coming steadily closer, yet remaining just beyond reach as if it were teasing her. The car had an automatic cruise control mechanism, which Carrie set for fifty-five miles an hour. The car briefly lurched forward before it settled on the designated speed. She bent her right leg under her left, and leaned back to relax in the plush velvet seat.

The car cruised steadily, heaving occasionally to cleave to the rolling grade of the road. She ate a little of the food, which she washed down with one of the beers. She became fully awake, bright-eyed and alert.

She had driven for a good fifty miles before she tried the radio. Among the hiss and crackling, she tuned in one country-western station after another, a few hard rock and roll. Disgusted, she shut it off.

At three-thirty in the afternoon, she went past another town that appeared as if out of nowhere in the desert. On the outskirts, she noted the arched entrance to a development of track homes, Land o'Lotus. It was a momentary respite in the bleakness of the desert, and no sooner did it appear than the terrain became flat and monotonous again.

The road was a newly constructed, stark, black ribbon. A gleaming yellow, broken stripe went along the middle and parallel white lines bordered both edges. The road shot straight ahead until its pinpoint disappeared far into the horizon.

As far off as Carrie Rasmussen could see, there was not another vehicle in sight. She steered the car with a long, manicured finger on the wheel, concentrating on staying in her lane as a way to prevent road hypnosis. The beer had given her a slight, sudden headache.

Then, the left rear tire blew.


At first she thought it might be a shift in the grade of the road that made the car swerve abruptly. It became more difficult to steer, forcing her to grip the wheel as it became stiff and unforgiving. She realized it couldn't be the road, as it was smoothly paved and even. She tapped the brake pedal to release the cruise control and allowed the car to slow on its own. The rumble beneath the car, as if someone were spanking it, confirmed her suspicions.

The car began to slow rapidly, and as it did so, it started to swerve more stubbornly, whipsawing. Carrie Rasmussen used all of her strength to keep a grip on the steering wheel. She managed to keep the car under control.

She waited until the car slowed considerably, moving along with a noisy thumping. When she felt it was safe, she pulled over onto the glistening white gravel shoulder. Her body shook as the car rolled to a stop. She opened the driver's door and was struck by a thick gust of hot desert wind. The sun reflected by the white gravel made her squint. As she stepped out of the car, another gust of wind ballooned the skirt of her dress over her thighs. She had but to glance at the left rear tire to confirm that it was flat.

Her mouth felt dry and uncomfortable.

"Fuck!" she said, aloud, angrily.


She looked back at the road she had travelled and saw not a vehicle moving. Neither was any vehicle coming from the direction in which she was going. Carrie scanned the horizon east and west in an involuntary plea for help. She gathered up her wits, reminded herself that there couldn't be much to changing a tire, even though she'd never changed one before.

She went back to the front seat of the car, sat down sideways, kept the door open, her feet on the ground. The engine idled and she noticed the noisy rush of conditioned air roaring out of the vents. She kept her feet on the ground. She reached behind her for the cigarettes on the adjacent seat. Carrie felt no great urgency to change the tire. She refused to be pressured by this small crisis.

She did feel the urge for another beer. Prudence told her to change the tire first. However, to change the tire, she would have to change clothes first. Her resolve to wait before having the beer lasted for only a few minutes. She'd drink the beer, and, maybe, while she drank it, someone might come along. She reached into the ice chest for a can of beer and popped it open.

She took a sip of the beer and looked across the road to a small ravine beyond which sand dunes began, white and plump like goose-bumps on the landscape. She remembered Chubby Johnson, the arche-typal prospector of the movies, leading his mule over grass speckled sand dunes. I wonder what that noise is, he would say, scratching his scraggly beard. While the audience shouted at the screen, don't go there, fool! Chubby Johnson would go behind a sand dune. A flying saucer would rise out of a cloud of dust, leaving in its wake the ashen outlines of Chubby Johnson and his faithful mule. Or, maybe he had his flesh sucked right off his bones by a giant tarantula, she couldn't remember exactly.

Carrie smiled thinly and took a long draught of the beer.

A little more of the beer to go before the can was empty. There was no telling when someone might come along, and if they did, they probably wouldn't stop. She was going to change the tire herself, there didn't seem to be an alternative. There was a pair of jeans and an old t-shirt in the suitcase. She finished the beer and tossed the empty can over the roof of the car into the sand and weeds. She made a plan. Change clothes, have another beer, change the tire, have another beer, hit the road.

She went around to the other side of the car and got into the back-seat from the passenger side. She opened the suitcase beside her. The jeans were rolled into a tube right on top. Carrie unzipped the dress in back and she raised up to slide the skirt of it over her hips. As she did so, she banged her knuckles on the car's roof as she brought the dress over her head.

"Goddamn it!" she said. After a pause, during which she sucked on her knuckle, she repeated, "Goddamn it, goddamn it, goddamn it!"

She dropped the dress on the floorboard and unrolled the jeans. Getting into them in the backseat was troublesome at first and finally impossible. She looked through the tinted windows again in both direc-tions for traffic. Seeing none, Carrie got out of the car. She wore only her red bikini underpants and the sandals.

She folded the dress carefully, packed it neatly in the suitcase. The few minutes in the sun caused her to perspire profusely. She wiped her brow. The scorching sun burned her bare skin. One of her bare breasts touched the metal of the door frame, searing it, and she cursed.

Hurriedly, she stepped into her jeans and as quickly she put on the t-shirt.

Dressed for the job, her confidence was renewed, she felt more in control of things. She took another beer, popped open the top. She leaned back in the seat to cool. When she'd finished the beer and tossed the empty away, Carrie went around to the rear of the car. She could not open the trunk without the keys that were in the ignition as the car idled.

She retrieved the keys, and opened the trunk to a momentary panic. She did not see a spare tire. She figured it must be under the imitation carpeting of the trunk. This she peeled to one side to reveal a crisp new tire. She bent over, pressed both of her hands to the tire, expecting it to be firm and plump. Carrie Rasmussen simply sighed in resignation when she discovered that the spare was flat, too.

Her arms felt damp and clammy. Her forehead was thoroughly wet. A bead of perspiration trickled down her cheek and dropped into a crease in her neck. A gust of warm desert air blew a strand of her hair, matting it to her dampened face. With miles and miles of Texas desert all around her, she slammed shut the trunk lid.

She came around to the driver's side of the car and got in. She started the engine and turned on the air conditioner full blast. What the hell, she thought, the gas tank needle still indicated close to a half tank. In a few minutes, the temperature inside the car became comfortable. She lowered the window an inch to keep the gas fumes from being trapped inside the car. She opened another beer.

"Shit!" said Carrie Rasmussen. She finished the beer, tossing the empty can among some dry twigs that sprouted out of the sand.

She opened another beer, she held it high up, tipped it in salute to an imaginary self just beyond the windshield. The imaginary figure sat, naked except for a pair of red bikini underpants, on the hot metal of the car's hood. She leaned against the car seat, flipping on the emergency blinkers, just in case someone drove by and might not otherwise notice she had a flat tire.

The trailer rig zooming by made Carrie jump up in the seat. The driver had seen her upending the beer can and had pulled the cord of the truck's horn, leaving a trailing sound that reminded her of the foghorns in Boston harbor. He had not stopped or even slowed. Carrie quickly opened the door and leaning out of the car, she waved to the driver. Again, she heard the horn. She kept watching the rig as it became a speck on the horizon and disappeared.

The rush of alcohol made her feel flushed and hot. A bloated feeling pushed against her bladder. Of course, she thought, that had to be next. Carrie walked around the hood of the car, opened the passenger door to shield her from an unlikely coming car. Facing the road she had travelled, she lowered her clothing to urinate. When she finished, she kicked dry sand over it. Back in the car, she opened another beer, brought her face to the air conditioner vent and let the stiff, cold air rush over her.

Carrie Rasmussen, drowsy from an alcoholic haze, insulated from outside sounds, did not notice the pickup truck that pulled up in back of the car. She had slumped deep into the seat. The radio was on and she was tapping her fingers on the steering wheel in time to the music, her eyes closed. The man's knuckles rapping on the window startled her. She turned her head, her eyes opened wide.

"Got trouble?" he asked, the sound of his voice muffled. It was a soft, friendly voice, accompanied by a deferent smile.

"Where did you come from?" Carrie said.

"I saw your lights flashing, ma'am. You have a tire looks flat. Can I help?" He said.

Carrie took her time before she gave her answer. She drew further into the car, gazing into the man's face.

"Yes, please. Thank you," said Carrie, after a long interval.

Out of a corner of her eye, Carrie saw the man grab the door handle. Frightened, she threw her hand on the padded window ledge, inches away from the lock latch.

"I need your keys, ma'am," said the man.

"My keys? Why?" asked Carrie, apprehensively.

"Get in the trunk. I have to get in the trunk. Spare tire. There's a spare tire, in there," he said.

"No, there isn't," said Carrie. "I mean, it's there, but it's flat, too."

"Are you sure? Have you checked?" he said, finding it hard to believe.

"Yes, I checked already."

"Well, do you want me to drive you somewhere to get it fixed?"

"No! I mean, I don't know."

"Alright, I understand, ma'am. I'm going up ahead and I'll tell them to come out and give you a hand. Should be a truck from Orange's Garage. Look for an orange truck. I'll tell them you need a tire. I'm just going to check on what size and I'll be on my way."

The man went around to the rear of the car and Carrie Rasmussen began to tremble with fear. The rear door was unlocked. She turned to watch him. All she saw was the man's head going out of sight as he bent down.

He stood up and began to walk toward the pickup. It was a brand new truck, black with thick red stripes, trimmed in lots of shiny chrome.

She heard the truck's engine kick over and shortly the truck eased up alongside the car. The window on the passenger side went down. He spoke to her without leaning over.

"You sure? You sure you don't want to come into town? Be no trouble. It might be better if you did, ma'am. Could be a while before anyone can come out to fix the tire." His voice was reassuring.

Carrie Rasmussen held up her left hand, palm out to indicate she wanted him to wait. She leaned over to gather up her purse and carkeys. She took the remaining pair of beer cans, still yoked in their plastic collars, and brought them with her.

Inside the man's truck it was icy cold. She offered him one of the beers.

"I don't drink, ma'am," he said, throwing the truck in gear and moving off into the highway.

"I'm sorry about what happened back there," Carrie said, trying to find something appropriate to say. Instead, she sipped the beer.

"That's alright. You were afraid, I guess. Lady lost in the middle of the road. I understand how you feel," he said, his eyes fixed on the road.

"I don't know what came over me," said Carrie. "I appreciate your help very much."

"It never hurts to be careful, ma'am. I always tell my own wife to be very careful every time she goes out. She never goes anywhere but just in town, you understand. Still, you can't be too careful, no matter where it is. You know?"

"I guess I should feel pretty silly."

"No, ma'am. You won't have anything to be afraid of, not anymore," the man said.


When he turned off the black ribbon of highway into a pair of ruts of an old mining road, Carrie Rasmussen turned her head suddenly.

"Where are you going?" asked Carrie, a streak of panic shooting through her. Her nipples pierced through the t-shirt.

"I thought we might stop, before going on into town."

He was polite, his voice soothing.

"What for? What is this? What are you doing?"

"You just behave yourself, that's all."

The man drove over a steep sand dune, with a long flat crest. About two hundred yards further he stopped the truck in the middle of a wide dry creek bed. He leaned across Carrie to open the glove compartment. The back of his head was inches from her face. She could smell a rancid hair tonic on his hair.

He took out a large hunting knife encased in a scabbard blackened from age and use. Holding it up, close to the windshield, the man unsheathed the knife. The sun glinted off its surface, striking Carrie in the face.

"Get out. I want you to take your clothes off," the man said, still polite, his voice quiet and unhurried.

Carrie Rasmussen began to tremble. She whimpered in tiny little squeals. Her lower lip vibrated. She tried several times to open the door until the man became irritated and impatient and yanked it open for her. Carrie stepped down, her foot sinking into the soft hot sand. She closed the door gently.

"Hurry up! Goddamn it!" the man shrieked, beginning to lose control.

She took a few steps toward the front of the truck. Quickly, she pulled the t-shirt over her head. She turned to face him, holding the garment to shield her breasts. Her eyes were full of tears, her hands trembling against her chin.

The man averted his head, trying not to look at her.

Carrie let go of the t-shirt and began to unbutton the jeans. She wiggled out of them, slowly, tossing them aside into the desert sand. Arms at her side, she stood before him in her red bikini underpants.

All of a sudden, Carrie was no longer afraid. A peacefulness and serenity came over her.

"The rest of it," the man said, his voice hoarse and thick.

Carrie hooked her thumbs on the waistband of the red bikini underpants. She began to turn slowly, giving him her back. Her chest flushed with goosebumps. She felt the presence of something, someone, behind her, moving toward her. She slid the panties over her round buttocks, down her thighs, and stopped at the knees. The figure, someone, something, came closer. She could feel the nearness of its presence. She spread her feet as wide apart as the straining material of the red bikini under pants permitted. She bent over and placed her hands on her knees.

Anytime now. She waited for the feel of cold steel penetrating her body.

# Rancho Notorious

The hues of the city became sharper as the airliner began its descent. The plane turned gradually in a graceful bank. The skyline of San Antonio appeared briefly, swathed in a diaphanous mist, pierced by diagonal streaks of autumn sunlight. It resembled a cluster of buildings enclosed in a crystal bubble. There was a slight shudder of the aircraft and the city disappeared from view. Below, miniature trees, house, and cars took shape.

George Doskovec was keen to every movement of the aircraft. As the plane got closer to the ground, he tightened his grip on the armrest. The ethereal sense of floating through space, buoyed by cloud masses, gave way to the imminent certainty of contact with the ground. He saw the rushing treetops through the porthole. In a few moments, it would be over.

Suddenly, as if there were no point in struggling to keep the aircraft aloft, there was a final, precipitous drop and a light thud as the tires brushed the tarmac. The craft bounced back up in the air for a second or two. George Doskovec's knuckles became white on the armrest. Again, the tires touched the tarmac and this time George felt the airplane gain purchase as it arched forward and accelerated.

George felt relieved to hear the deafening roar of the engines fanned to slow the airplane. His head came off the headrest as the pilot applied the brakes. George began to relax, his breathing became easier. He let go of the armrest.

"We're here, George," said Myrna Doskovec, patting the back of his hand to reassure him.

George Doskovec turned to see his wife applying lipstick, squinting in a compact mirror. She inspected her face by swivelling it from side to side. Satisfied with what she saw, she exhaled, clicked the compact shut, and dropped it into the gaping purse in her lap.

"Look out there! Look at the wide open spaces," Myrna said sarcastically, leaning over him to get closer to the window.

The plane made a sharp, right-angle turn and the airport terminal came into view. The only wide open spaces to be seen were airport property.

"I don't know why you are so afraid of flying, George," said Myrna. "It's safer than driving a car, you know."

The din of the passengers began before the plane came to a complete stop, as they unbuckled their seatbelts and started to rummage in the overhead storage compartments for their carry-on luggage. George Doskovec, still not fully recuperated from the strain of the flight, remained seated. He would be one of the last stragglers to exit, a habit which irritated Myrna.

As the plane began to empty out, George and Myrna got their things and walked through the first class section to where a small group of people bottlenecked at the exit. The stewardess stood patiently beside the door with the frozen undulation of a smile.

A shaft of warm air struck George as he stepped off the plane onto a passenger chute that imperfectly connected with the skin of the aircraft. At the end of the chute he was enveloped by the comfortable air conditioning of the terminal.

George and Myrna entered the terminal proper. The crowd of people waiting for arriving passengers had already thinned out. Those who remained were anxious, more expectant, rising on the balls of their feet as they caught the first glimpses of the people coming out of the chute. As they came out of the chute, they were greeted by fading smiles on the scattered faces.

George, who was a step in front of Myrna, stopped to look over the terminal. The brochure in the breastpocket of his suit jacket indicated that someone would be there to greet them and to take them out to Rancho Notorious.

Seeing no one, George and Myrna began the agitated walk of New Yorkers along a lengthy concourse lined with paintings for sale, many of which depicted wild west scenes.

At the end of the concourse, off to one side, George asked a lady in the information booth about transportation to the area dude ranches. He was told to go outside and look for a station wagon or a van with the name of the dude ranch he wanted painted on the side. George thanked the woman and repeated the information to Myrna even though she had been right beside him and had already heard it.


Outside of the terminal, in the stench of exhaust fumes, they could feel the warmth of the bright sun. The air, though, had a slight chill to it. George's wool suit was a little too heavy for the weather, but it kept him from shivering as little gusts of air struck his fleshy cheeks. Myrna wore a scarlet cashmere coat, inside of which she appeared prim and warm.

An assortment of people waiting for transportation surrounded them. Servicemen not as yet at ease in their first-issue uniforms, older men with close-cropped hair wearing pointed-toe boots, a few women in fur coats. Next to the curb was a phalanx of idling taxis and private cars. Across the street, people walked to and from a dense parking lot.

Myrna spotted the van first. It was painted a dirty white beneath the coating of dust, dented in places, pockmarked, and streaked with rusty nicks and scratches. A young man whose appearance was equally shabby, leaned against the snubbed hood of the van, talking with a police officer. His hair came over his shoulders in a frayed, scraggly curtain beneath a sweat-stained brown cowboy hat. His cowboy boots were scuffed. The cuffs of his jeans were so frayed that they became fringe around the heels of the boots.

"He must be ours, George," said Myrna, indicating with a toss of her head so as not to take her hands out of her pockets. "That one over there."

"Rancho Notorious, that's us," said George Doskovec, reading the lettering on the side of the van. Above the letters, faded but still discernible, were the faces of Marlene Dietrich, Mel Ferrer and Arthur Kennedy.

"You wait here, Myrna."

George walked through the maze of waiting cars up to the young man, who waved a salute to the departing policeman. George spoke with him for a few seconds and came back.

"Go on over to the van. I'll get the luggage," George said, stooping to gather up their carry-on bags.

"Well, isn't he going to help you, George," said Myrna, who had not moved. She did little to mask her impatience.

"He can't leave the van unattended, Myrna. That's what the sign there says. A policeman just warned him about it."

George hurried to deposit the bags on the pavement below the sliding doors of the van. He retraced his steps, giving Myrna a hapless, wistful smile as he walked by her to go into the terminal for the luggage they had checked in.

"With me in the vehicle, it wouldn't be unattended, George," said Myrna, her voice trailing to a whisper when she realized he couldn't hear her.

Myrna moved reluctantly past the idling cars. She stopped next to the passenger door of the van. The young man leaned against the front of the van, the heel of his boot hooked over the rusted bumper. Shaking her head in disgust, Myrna jerked open the door. The young man, startled by the sound of it, came suddenly to life. He scurried around and threw open the sliding door.

"I think you probably want to ride back here, ma'am," he drawled, "that way, you and your husband, ya'll can sit together."

Myrna glared at him. She slammed shut the passenger door. She might have said something, had not George appeared carrying their two out-sized suitcases.

"You might help my husband," Myrna said evenly, keeping herself under control.

"Yes, ma'am," the young man said.

The long-haired young man walked up to George Doskovec and took the two suitcases. Without a word, he placed them in a storage compartment in back of the van. When he finished, he came around on the other side to get into the driver's seat.

There were three padded benches behind the driver's seat. George and Myrna Doskovec chose the middle one. The interior, mottled with rust spots, was acutely cold and it smelled of rotting hay, oil and grease, and horse hair upholstery. The engine sputtered for a little bit and then the driver gunned it, making a loud roar.

"You folks strapped in?" asked the young man.

"No," said George.

"Well, I sure wish you would. Company policy," he said, trying to make eye contact in the rearview mirror.

Without waiting to verify that they had buckled their seatbelts, the young man threw the van in gear and it lurched forward. The policeman, to whom he had been talking, stopped traffic so the van could merge in.

At the end of the airport boulevard, the driver turned right into a feeder that brought him into the Loop that girds San Antonio. The van roared reluctantly to pick up speed and the young man soon enough shuffled in with the freeway traffic. He drove for a few miles along the Loop and took the exit marked Leon Valley.

"How far is it to where we're going?" asked Myrna.

"It's a ways, yet, ma'am," said the young man. "This is just the road that goes out to Bandera. We'll be going through Leon Valley and Helotes. Just more San Antonio, if you ask me."

It was forty-five miles to Bandera, according to the sign which George noticed. They drove for a good fifteen minutes flanked by strip shopping centers, industrial parks, franchise restaurants, clogged inter-sections, and housing subdivisions.

As they got further out into the fringes of metropolitan San Antonio, the driver informed them that they were now in Helotes. Immediately to his left, he indicated John T. Floore's Country Store, which he claimed was legendary in Texas country music. The information meant nothing to George and Myrna Doskovec.

The van rattled noisily. The springs in the benchseats gave very little. George and Myrna jiggled, swayed and bounced like puppets. It helped that they were tethered to the bench by the seatbelts.

Once out of Helotes, the van chugged up a lenient grade in the road. On the other side, they swept into a panoramic vista of hump-backed hills and graceful valleys. The hills were dappled with patches of green treetops.

George Doskovec was taken aback by what he had seen of Texas thus far. The drive from the airport was turning out to be far longer and more unpleasant than he had expected. The dude ranch brochure, presented to them by a travel agent in Queens, gushed about a brief scenic drive along Old West trails that had once been the route for cattle drives. Cowboy and gunfighter country, the brochure copy exclaimed. So where are the cowboys, thought George, where are the cattle? So far, in one of the valleys, he had seen three maybe four cows grazing.

"Look at that," George, said Myrna. "Is this the Old West? Where is the desert?"

"We're just at the outskirts of the city, Myrna," said George, betraying a little irritation. Myrna drew a small comfort from the fact that she and George were thinking the same thing. Myrna pressed her lips together in a thin smile.

"Ya'll want to hear some music?" the driver asked.

Without waiting for a response, he flicked on the radio. He glanced at his passengers in the rearview mirror. The young man increased the volume, as if acceding to their wishes. He moved in the driver's seat, rolling his shoulders, bobbing his head, tapping the steering wheel in time to the rock and roll that screeched from the tiny distorting speaker.

George Doskovec asked the driver to lower the volume, please. The driver did not hear him. Not wishing to raise his voice, George unbuckled the seatbelt and in a wobbly crouch, duckwalked forward to tap the driver on the shoulder. Again, he asked that the volume be lowered, please.

"Yeah, sure," said the young man.

Although George saw him comply with his request, there was no appreciable lessening of the crackling, distorted noise. George wanted to ask the young man some questions, questions about what it was like at the dude ranch. There was no point to it, he decided, it wouldn't be possible to talk above the noise of the radio.

"Some Old West, George! Where are the cowboys," began Myrna Doskovec. They were rounding a curve carved out of the side of a fat lumpy hill. It was a two-tiered road, the oncoming lanes several feet below. The van was straining to roll up the steep incline of the curve.

George Doskovec settled back in his seat, wishing that Myrna would not start. She was ready to start, he could tell. Even before they boarded the plane at Kennedy, she had been ready. He had ignored her as best he could and she had let it drop. Only, Myrna didn't just let it drop. She'd save it.

George groped for something to say, hoping that a civil answer might restrain her, prolong the inevitable.

"We'll get there, to the ranch," he said, and leaned back, draping his neck over the backrest.

"Suppose this ranch is nothing but a motel by the side of the road in the middle of nowhere, George," said Myrna. "What then?"

"Myrna, be reasonable," said George.

"I don't know where you came up with this idea for a vacation, George," said Myrna. It had started. She was on her way and there was no way to stop her. Luckily, the driver would not overhear.

"We've taken the same vacation for sixteen years. Where did you get the idea to be different this year?"

"It wasn't my idea, Myrna. We won this trip. We discussed it several times, or so I thought, and we agreed that it might be fun to have a change. We agreed that we would make the best of it and that we would try to have a good time. We agreed, Myrna!" Toward the end, his syllables were short and clipped, forceful. George sighed and hoped it was enough to get her to drop it.

"We still should have gone to Mystic Seaport as we do every year, George," said Myrna Doskovec.

"We could have gone to Yugoslavia, Myrna," said George. "I've never been back to visit the place where I was born."

"We don't know the language, George."

"I remember enough of it," said George.

"I don't know why we didn't go to Mystic Seaport. Sam and Dorothy are close by in Bridgeport. They're such nice people. They always invite us to dinner, George."

"I like Sam and Dorothy," said George, sincerely. "They always have nice dinners for us."

"You can say that again, George. And, don't forget Aunt Ernestine. We could stay at her house, George, any time we want, instead of having to pay for motels and guest cottages. But you won't make an effort to get her to like you. She's never liked you. That's not like you, George. You're a very likable man. Complete strangers take to you right away. In a matter of seconds, you make life-long friends. I don't know why Aunt Ernestine doesn't like you. If she did, she'd invite us to stay with her."

"Your aunt Ernestine's house is a museum, Myrna. There's no room for us. All she has is a small apartment."

"It's such a big house," said Myrna, drifting into her own recollections. "I remember it when I was a little girl."

Myrna paused to look at the countryside rolling by. She was a descendent of New England sea captains. She had the stern face of women who spend their lives waiting for the return of seafaring husbands. Myrna's father had been an officer on a merchantman. The months and years away at sea were nothing more than family lore. Myrna's father was away from home no more than a week at a time, serving a milkrun between Boston and New York. Nevertheless, it was a tradition among the women in her family. Myrna had been brought up to be proud of it.

Momentarily, Myrna was back in the present.

"We could have breakfast on the veranda, in the cool of the morning, before the tourists come in. Just like the last time we visited. Remember Aunt Ernestine sitting there. White linen tablecloth and the silver tea service. Real silver, George, not plated. It's been in the family for generations. She's like a queen, my Aunt Ernestine. We could be sitting there with her this year. Be the envy of all those tourists. Wouldn't that be something?"

"All I remember," said George, "is having to pay to get past that young girl who collected the admissions."

"That was not one of your better moments, George, I don't mind telling you," Myrna said. "When you insisted to the poor thing that relatives don't have to pay to visit relatives. She got red as a cranberry. She was just doing her job."

"It wasn't the money, Myrna. Every year I send a contribution to the museum."

"I know, George, you became stubborn over the principle of the thing. Your principle created quite a disturbance, as I remember," said Myrna, sarcastically. "We were lucky they didn't call the police."

"All your Aunt Ernestine had to do was walk over and straighten the whole thing out. She was right there. But, she didn't. She sat there, sipping her tea, as if she enjoyed watching our discomfort. Maybe she did want me to be arrested," said George.

"That's probably true. I already told you, she doesn't like you, George," Myrna said, smugly.

"Well, for your sake, then," said George. "She could have done something."

Myrna Doskovec remained silent. George felt oddly eager to continue, but he kept his silence, too.

The driver, head bobbing to the music, had not heard any of their conversation. He was concentrating mostly on the music and once in a while on the road. It had been long minutes since they'd met an oncoming car.

In a clearing, perhaps a mile wide, surrounded by limestone hills studded with pine and oak, George saw the entrance to a ranch. In the distance, at the foot of the hills, he could make out the shapes of four people on horseback.

"Over there, Myrna, see? Cowboys! That's what we came for," said George.

"Four people on horses. They might be tourists just like us. I wouldn't call that the Old Wild West, George," said Myrna.

"It's picturesque, that's what I meant, Myrna. See how they're so small with that hill in the background?" George said.

Myrna thought for a moment and took a deep breath. The result was an elaborate sigh, exaggerated for George's benefit.

"What are we going to do here for two weeks? If we have to sleep out in the woods, out in the open, sleeping bags or no sleeping bags, I'm going home. I'm warning you, George, if I see one sleeping bag, I catch the next plane."

"It'll be fine, Myrna," said George. "You'll see. We just have to give it a chance. If you could just bring yourself to give it a chance. That's all. It's not asking too much to give it a chance."

"Well, I want to go to the bathroom, George," Myrna said. "How much longer before we get there?"

"Why didn't you go at the airport, Myrna," said George, regretting instantly that he said anything.

"I didn't need to go at the airport. Besides, you know how it acts up when I'm not comfortable. And I am anything but comfortable right now."

George Doskovec unbuckled his seatbelt, and crouched forward, holding on to the backrest of the bench in front. He sat on it, leaning forward to tap the driver on the shoulder.

"Excuse me," said George to the young man driving, "how long before we get to the ranch?"

He twisted his head to yell at the top of his voice, "We're just a minute to Bandera, mister." He turned quickly to correct his steering. Sensing that George had not moved, he added, "after that, then it's maybe another ten minutes out to the ranch. Ain't too far."

George Doskovec returned to his wife. When he was strapped in his seat, he tapped her knee reassuringly.

"We're almost there, Myrna," he said. "You can go in town."

"Look over there, George, it's a Pizza Hut!" said Myrna, scornfully, as houses and businesses began to crop up more densely. "We could be in the part of Connecticut that connects to New York!"

Bandera was an uneasy combination of the old and the new. In New England, Yankee entrepreneurs and city fathers worked hand in hand to blend in new buildings in the style and the feel of the old. Here, there was the sense of cross purposes.

There were those who traded upon cowboy history, most notably the symbol of the cowboy as refashioned in movies. And then there were those, perhaps truer to the wild west spirit, who sold small tracts of land that promised a respite from other people. The time was long past when a man could push beyond the limits of civilization and make of himself what he could, living off the land, drawing upon his own physical resources. For those who struck it rich in Dallas, in Houston, in San Antonio, Bandera provided the reward of a small ranch or a riverfront cabin, where, for a weekend, or a week, or a month, they could live out the fantasy of the frontier.

It was these two interests that competed with each other at the cross-roads in Bandera. The only thing to sell is image, thought George. It shouldn't be too difficult to get everyone to contribute to the common-weal. Curiously, the strength of the images evinced a defiance to the common purpose.

The young driver slowed the van as he came up to the stop sign. The ride became smoother, the rattling lessened, but the roar of the engine seemed greater. He turned off the radio.

"Bandera," announced the driver, superfluously. "To your right is the cowboy capital of the world."

Through his half-closed eyes, George peered through the windshield as the driver made a right turn into a short block of false-front buildings. Souvenir shops and restaurants. The merchandise hung on the tall windows and overflowed into the sidewalks. The objects of the Old West, a symbolic detritus, took the form of souvenirs. It had the appearance of an authentic movie set.

"There's a saloon in there," the driver said, "if you gotta go or you want a beer."

"I don't know, George," said Myrna, leaning over on his shoulder. "I'm feeling better. Just a little tired. I can wait."

"Just go on," said George Doskovec. "We're tired. We're anxious to get out to the ranch."

"You folks gonna need anything before we get to the ranch?" the young man asked. "This'll be the place to get it. You know, toothpaste, soap, towels, whatever you mighta forgot. Up ahead are some stores."

"We don't need anything," said George.

"Whatever you say," the driver said. "Some folks is used to just driving to the store on the corner when they need something. Never fails. Get out on the ranch, you find you forgot something. Then you find out it ain't like back home. Out here, there ain't nothing on the corner except more road."

"We're fine," said George, "if you could get us to the ranch, thank you."

The driver rolled through the main street at a snail's pace, the engine sputtering as he down shifted. He lowered his window all the way down and hooked an elbow over the frame. His head was out the window as he looked at people on the sidewalk. The air inside the van became chilly. Myrna shivered and drew her shoulders together.

At the end of the street, the young man gunned the engine several times before he threw it into gear and speeded up on the way out of town. He glanced at them in the rearview mirror every time he shifted gears.

"Ya'll doing alright?" he asked.

In a few minutes they were out of Bandera, descending along a narrow road. The blacktop cut across rivulets that flowed from the hills above. The runoff collected along trenches on either side of the road. They came upon several stretches of road where the large oaks on either side spliced their branches to form a canopy.

The driver shifted gears to slow the van. The billboard announcing Rancho Notorious was nailed to two pine posts inserted into an oval clearing on the passenger side of the road. The slightly faded lettering was in bold block letters, colored in orange and brown. On the right side of the billboard was a badly drawn likeness of Marlene Dietrich that stopped right where her cleavage began. The two figures on either side of her bore no resemblance at all to Arthur Kennedy and Mel Ferrer, Marlene Dietrich's costars in the movie, *Rancho Notorious*.

The young man slowed to negotiate a sharp right turn onto a rocky limestone road. Rancho Notorious was still five miles away. The going on this leg of the journey was more precarious as the road was little more than twin ruts that see-sawed along the terrain. At one place, the young man slowed the van to a crawl to traverse a foot of water flowing over the road.

"We had a little rain a while back," the young man said, tossing the words over his shoulder. "Sometimes, you misjudge the force of the water and you end up where you don't need to be at all."


The road ended between two pine poles that flanked the entrance to Rancho Notorious. Beyond the entrance was a smooth driveway of finely crushed gravel. A white-washed fence fanned out to circle the property. To one side stood a corral whose railings were painted in red primer. About a dozen horses grazed on scattered hay bales inside the corral.

For the first time since leaving Kennedy, George Doskovec felt at ease with the decision to accept the vacation out west. The spread before him was not quite as authentic-looking as ranches he saw in the movies. Still, the layout provided an overall impression that was satisfactory to him. It was peaceful and scenic. Once into the thick of things, participating in the guest activities listed by the brochure, George Doskovec thought, even Myrna would like it.

The van came to stop in front of the main building. At the airport, George had not expected the flush of heat tinged with chilly wind. Here, higher up in the hills, it was cooler, the air thinner, and the sun felt delicate and gentle on the skin.

The longhaired driver went around to get their bags. George and Myrna stepped inside the main building. Immediately to their right was a formica-top counter set upon angled iron poles. In front of them, straight ahead, through a set of glass double-doors, George saw what resembled a spacious living room. He decided it was much too large for a living room. The distance between the items of furniture, set at angles to square Navajo rugs, made the space much too arid and cold.

Navajo rugs hung on walls to the left and right, like tapestries. Next to the rugs on one wall were three cow's skulls hanging in a vertical row. On either side of them hung two sets of criss-crossed scythes and tomahawks.

On the opposite wall, behind a beige leather sofa, paintings of Indians, horses, cowboys, and buffalo framed the blanket. There was a space of some five feet between the sofa and the wall where a person could pace and study the paintings. A bronze sculpture of a horse and rider sat on a pedestal in the corner.

George walked to the counter and leaned his elbows on it. The place seemed deserted. Myrna Doskovec remained close by the door to wait for the longhair to bring in their luggage. When the young man set it just outside the door, Myrna remained standing where she could see it.

"He ain't heard you yet?" the young man said, walking around Myrna. He came up to the counter and rapped on it sharply. "Ben! You got guests, Ben!" He turned to George and explained, "Ole Ben gets busy these days."


"Welcome to Rancho Notorious," said the tall, sun-burned man, who came out of an office behind the counter. "Hope I haven't kept you waiting too long. We're fixing to close up the place for the season. For good, I should say. You'll be our last guests."

"The travel agent didn't mention anything about that," said George.

"I think it's something we should have been told."

"You're probably right. You should have been told," said the man, continuing, "had anyone known about it, that is. As it is, no one is supposed to know. It won't be official for a few weeks, yet."

He reached into his shirt pocket with an absent-minded air to take out a pair of reading glasses. He positioned them at the tip of his nose. He wrinkled his nose, arched his eyebrows, as he began to sift through a pile of papers.

"Let's see, here. That would make you Mr. and Mrs. George Doskovec, from New York. Right?"

He stuck his hand out for George to shake.

"Yes," said George.

"Ellsworth. Benjamin Ellsworth. Pleased to make your acquaintance, Mr. Doskovec."

After George let go of his hand, Benjamin Ellsworth waved to Myrna, who had not moved from the entrance.

"Miz Doskovec, nice to meet you, too," said Benjamin Ellsworth, waving some more.

"Can I have the rest of the day, Ben?" asked the young man.

"Way you ask, Doug, you don't want me to dock you for it, either, do you?" said Benjamin Ellsworth, smiling tolerantly.

The long haired young man, Doug, lowered his head to look at the tips of his toes. Ellsworth began to sift through his papers again.

"Get the van in good shape, in case Mr. and Mrs. Doskovec need it tonight. Then you can go. Full pay. What do you say?" he asked.

"Thanks, Ben," said Doug, going out in a hurry, throwing out 'preciate it,' over his shoulder.

"It's good to be reminded of what it's like to be young, isn't it?" said Benjamin Ellsworth, smiling.

"What's this about closing down, Mr. Ellsworth," George asked.

"Ben. Call me, Ben," said Benjamin Ellsworth. "We've closed everything up, except for the one cabin where you'll be staying. It's the Gabby Hayes Suite. You remember Gabby Hayes?"

"Sure," said George, "rode with Roy Rogers and Hopalong Cassidy."

"One and the same," said Benjamin Ellsworth, making rapid notations on a three-by-five card. "Sign here, please, Mr. Doskovec."

George Doskovec signed the card and slid it back to Ellsworth. Ellsworth made a cursory check of the card and dropped it into a wooden box. He took a folded letter out of his pocket, tapped the formica counter several times with it. As he started to speak, he placed both elbows on the counter.

"I had a hell of a time staying open to accommodate your stay here. My attorneys wanted me to hand you over to one of the neighbors. Thing is, most of them close for the season, too, this time of year. Seeing as I had no choice, we'll do everything we can to help you enjoy yourselves," Benjamin Ellsworth said.

He reached under the counter for an envelope into which he stuffed the letter. He slid the flap inside the envelope and placed it in front of George Doskovec.

"If you'd read this, sign it and return it to me before you leave, I'd be grateful. It confirms that you stayed here, how long, that sort of thing. I made a deal for these trips. You'll be the last one. That letter will get me paid."

"I see," said George, becoming a little more apprehensive. "Is anything wrong? What I'm getting at, should my wife and I know a little more than what you've told us?"

"I don't think so. I don't want you to be alarmed. The long and short of it, Mr. Doskovec, is, I'm bankrupt," Ellsworth said. "My attorney filed the papers yesterday."

"So, you're closing up permanently?"

"That's right, Mr. Doskovec. We're working out an agreement with my creditors. There's no point in trying to stay open. There's little likelihood that I can make a go of this place. In view of how things stand, I don't see where anyone would want to take over." Benjamin Ellsworth took a deep breath. "I have to face the inevitable, Mr. Doskovec."

"I'm sorry to hear that, Ben," said George, "I'm in business myself, I know how you must feel."

"It happens, George," said Benjamin Ellsworth, brightening up and smiling. He came around the edge of the counter, sweeping his arm out in the direction of the next room. "It's our custom, by the way, to have drinks with our new guests."

"My wife would be interested in a bathroom, before anything else," George said as they paced along.

Ellsworth shook Myrna's hand and pointed.

"It's right down that hallway there," he said.

"What about the bags," said Myrna.

"They'll be fine just where they are," said Ellsworth. "I'll get someone to help you with the bags when you're ready."

Myrna glanced at George, reluctant to leave the bags unattended. George nodded to her that it would be okay. Life in New York was a constant vigil and she frowned at George to let him know that he shouldn't be so gullible. Shaking her head, Myrna moved on in the direction of the bathroom, along a cream-colored hallway lined with paintings.

Benjamin Ellsworth went ahead to a corner of the large room to pull the drawcord for the drapes of a plateglass window that ran the length of the room. A vista of trees and hills appeared just beyond the swimming pool in the foreground.

"I'll fix some drinks," said Ellsworth. "What'll it be, George?"

"Beer for me. My wife will have a Tab."

"How about Diet Pepsi? That's all there is."

"I'm sure that'll be fine," said George.

Benjamin Ellsworth brought over a drink caddy that resembled a bar on rollers. George had a glimpse of the rows of bottles and a small white cooler on a shelf underneath. Ben positioned the caddy in front of the plate glass windows.

"Yes, it is. I wish the swimming pool was elsewhere. I always told myself if I could make this place a success, I'd move it. Hang the expense," Ellsworth talked as he placed a bottle of beer on the top of the caddy, and he bent down again to search for the Pepsi.

"You'll have to excuse me, George," said Ellsworth, "I have to go find some ice. Your beer is right here. Don't stand on ceremony, please."

"I will, Ben. And, thanks," said George.

George Doskovec went up to the bar and leaned over on his elbows, his shoulders hunched close together. He took a long swallow directly from the beer bottle and looked at the view that seemed to sweep up to the concrete lip of the swimming pool. His eyes became fixed on a spot beyond the purple crests of three fat and puffy hills.

Myrna's short clipped steps from one direction and Ellsworth's longer heavier steps from the other brought George out of his reverie. Ellsworth carried a plastic bucket full of ice.

Myrna came up beside her husband. Ellsworth used ice tongs to fill two glasses with cubes. He pulled the tab on the can of soda and set can and glass in front of Myrna. Ellsworth took a bottle of Artesia sparkling water for himself.

"Here's to you, our last and most special guests," said Benjamin Ellsworth, raising his glass in a toast. George raised his beer bottle, tipped it toward Ellsworth. Myrna poured her soda, but did not bother to return the toast.

"Gabby Hayes is a strange name for a cabin, isn't it?" asked George.

"I can't say that I've thought about it," said Benjamin Ellsworth. "The other cabins are named Walter Brennan, Smiley Burnette, Pat Buttram, Fuzzy St. John, Fuzzy Knight—we call those Fuzzy one and Fuzzy two—Raymond Hatton, Pat Brady, and Andy Devine."

"Don't you see what those names have in common?" said George, genuinely curious.

"They were actors in cowboy movies, I know that much," said Ellsworth. "I've tried to watch cowboy movies on the satellite but I don't have the patience for it."

"They were all sidekicks," said George, emphatically. "Each one was paired with one of the great cowboys as a sidekick."

"Yes, I suppose you're right, George. I don't know very much about western movies," said Ellsworth, apologetically. "There's an eight by ten glossy of each of those gentlemen hanging in the cabin that bears his name."

"Amazing," said George. "I wonder who thought of it."

"I bought this place four years ago. When I came here, I decided to leave things the way they were. It was good for my health and good for our repeat business. Build on a winning formula, but don't fiddle too much with it."

"The brochure we received said that this is a working cattle ranch," said George.

"Probably was, at one time. It's been Rancho Notorious since '53, '54. The original owner probably couldn't survive the post-war depression. Or, maybe he just got fed up with ranching. Not the easiest way to make a living. As far as this being a working cattle ranch, well, you said you were in business. You must understand about marketing. A little fact can go a long way."

"I was expecting to see a working cattle ranch," said George.

"There's cattle ranches in the area. I could arrange for you and your wife to visit one. Won't be much to see, this time of year. Besides, they use four-wheel drive vehicles, now, helicopters, airplanes, that sort of thing. I don't think they get up on horses unless they absolutely have to. Only time I see people on horseback is during a parade."

"You have a lot of horses here."

"Oh, yes. For our guests. I'm about to send them to auction. Probably right after you leave. In the meantime, you'll get your share of horseback riding. Not enough so you'll despise it like the cowboys do, but you'll get your share."

"So, this is just another hotel with horses," said George.

"It's been reduced to that, George. In another month, it'll just be real estate up for sale."


George Doskovec picked up his beer and walked around the caddy right up to the glass wall. He began to stare at the open country. He spoke softly, just loud enough for his wife and Ellsworth to hear.

"My father came to America as a refugee from Eastern Europe, right after the war. I was five years old. We came over on a cargo ship.

There weren't very many passengers. My father took me on deck to look at the ocean one day. We were on the bow of the ship and my father had to pick me up so I could look over the side. The pitch of the ship was terrifying. The bow would rise up slowly and then suddenly drop so fast that it seemed to me we were going under. The water seemed so close I could almost reach out and touch it. I became more terrified because I couldn't see land. I wanted off the ship. I wanted to run. But there was no place to run, nothing to run on. I've never forgotten how terrified I became on the deck of that ship. Even today, I become terrified when I know there isn't solid ground under my feet. If I go higher than the third story of a building I start to get hot and my hands begin to sweat."

"You flew out here," Ellsworth reminded him.

"I'll fly. I won't be crippled by my terror," said George, pausing briefly. "We settled in an area of New York with others from our country. My father opened a small shop. He was so proud when he was able to lease the shop, that he went around showing the contract to everybody. I think he took more pride in leasing the place than he did years later when he bought it."

"George," said Myrna, interrupting. "We ought to go freshen up. It's been a long day."

George continued. "My father had a knack for putting things together again. Even things he'd never seen before, he could figure out how they were supposed to work and fix what was wrong. Mostly, though, he put handles back on pots, patching things, that sort of thing. He started doing things as a favor for the other refugees. They gave him what they thought his work was worth. It was just like back in the old country. He had lots of friends. That small shop my father had was a place where our friends came to sit around and talk. That's what I most remember about it.

"Sometimes, I'd come by after school to listen to them talk in the old language. They'd explain some of the words to me when they thought I wouldn't understand. There was always a pot of coffee on and I was glad when they'd ask me to pour for them. My mother would send me to the shop with a tray of hot rolls, or bread, or sweetcakes. There were wonderful smells in my father's shop, what with the coffee and the breads and the smoke from their cigarettes, and my father's welding equipment and oils and sweet-smelling glues.

"My father's reputation grew beyond our neighborhood. When he asked his customers to pay what they thought the work was worth, they became uncomfortable. He set prices and no one objected. Pretty soon, we moved out of the apartment to a house.

"By the time i was in high school, the shop had become a plant. The special corner of the shop where our friends gathered was gone, made

into an office for the foreman he hired. My father no longer fixed things
for which he got paid in coins. He got orders from factories, some in
New York, others upstate. I don't think he ever knew the people he did
business with. He sent out invoices and he received checks in return.
Our friends were all gone. When I began to work there after school and
summers, I realized that it had become a lonely place for my father."

George had finished his beer and Ellsworth opened another for him,
which he placed on the bar. George took his time before he drank from
it.

"You took over your father's business, then?" Benjamin Ellsworth
asked.

"My father's business? I don't know if I could call it that. I read
papers all day. My secretary types papers for me. I talk to people on
the phone and somehow the conversation ends up on paper. My book-
keeper puts my salary in the bank. I don't even see a check.

"When my father ran the business, I would work at least half a day
on the line. Shoulder to shoulder with the workers. They knew I didn't
have to. I could have sat in my office all day, not gotten dirty at all. They
respected my father for the way he had built up the business. He was
like a father to them. I wanted that kind of respect for myself. When
my father died and I had to take over the company, I noticed a change
right away in the attitude of the employees. Before, I could fit right in
with them. After, it was like something came between us, a line that
neither of us, not I and not them, could cross.

"I wasn't my father's kid anymore . It didn't matter that I had worked
alongside of them ever since I could remember. In my own way, I had
put as much into the company as they had. In the end, I became the
faceless boss upstairs. I go out on the plant floor for retirement parties
and immediately there is a change in their attitude. Some of the men
were those I poured coffee for, men I had served my mother's pastries.
The younger ones were kids I played with."

"Things change, George, it's human nature," said Benjamin Ellsworth.

"I'm telling you this, Ben, because things have worked out for me
exactly as I always thought they would," said George, pausing for a sip
of his beer. "There's been very little change that I have not predicted
or expected."


Benjamin Ellsworth regarded the contents of the near empty glass
of bottled water, before speaking.

"I was going along, same as you, until I had my heart attack," said
Benjamin Ellsworth. "When it was over, when I had recuperated to the

point where I no longer was scared to death, my doctor said it was a warning attack. He put it as plainly as it can be put. Change my life or die.

"At the age of forty-four, my doctor suggested I quit. Junk everything, start over and go on to something else. A friend who knew I was looking for a business opportunity put me on to this place. What with terrorism and an uncertain dollar abroad, I figured a dude ranch might provide a leisurely living for me."

"Seems like a perfectly quiet life out here," said George.

"I came out here without a clue as to what to expect. To begin with, I was never taken with western lore or cowboy movies. It was a business venture and nothing more.

"It turns out that I'm selling nostalgia. There's not much profit in this kind of nostalgia, though. It's a controlled self-reliance. Vacationers, I've discovered, prefer to be pampered. Everything at their fingertips. I can't afford a full complement of servants.

"You figure, you're on a ranch, you can't have all the conveniences. Most people find that this isn't what they expected but they get used to it. In the end, though, they want more. That's the part I regret, I never felt healthy enough to give it the drive it needed. I saw myself falling into the same habits as before. I had to pull back to stay alive."

"You chose your life over your business," offered George.

"I guess you could say that," said Benjamin Ellsworth in a tired voice.

"What'll you do now?"

"Move down the road, as they say, into San Antonio. The weather's better there," he said, jokingly.

Myrna Doskovec had remained quiet, taking only tiny sips of her soft drink. She stood rigid and erect at the bar, clutching her purse tightly between her upper arm and her ribs.

"You say we'll be the only ones here? What's that going to be like," asked Myrna.

"That's hard to say," Ellsworth said. "Depends on how you take to being alone. Some people like it that way, some don't. Solitude does different things to different people. Of course, there's plenty of social things to do in Bandera if you need the company of people. There's Kerrville to the east and San Antonio to the south, about an hour to either."

"What about the things promised in your brochure? Or, are they also facts that can go a long way," said George, expressing his understanding in a smile.

"We've closed down most of our facilities. The horses are still here, as you saw. I had planned to drain the pool today, but if you'll make use of it, it can wait. No hurry. It's chilly most mornings, but it gets fairly warm in the afternoon, warm enough for a brisk swim. Food is included in your package. I've arranged for you to take your meals at any of the restaurants in town. The van is yours to use. I can provide a driver, if you desire. I rather suspect you'll want to go off by yourselves."

"That might be interesting," said George, optimistically.

"George," implored Myrna.

"Excuse me," said Benjamin Ellsworth.

He walked diagonally across the room, through the double doors and disappeared into the cubicle that served as the front desk. After a moment they heard the blare of a loudspeaker outside. "Doug, come to the desk!"

A few minutes later, the long haired young man who had been their driver came running in, out of breath.

"Take the bags to Gabby Hayes, will you, Doug."

"Yes, sir, Ben," the young man said and began picking up the bags. He had one bag under his arm and another suspended from his hand when Myrna noticed and came running.

"Wait for us!" she yelled.

"I hope you enjoy your stay," said Benjamin Ellsworth, as George and Myrna followed the dog.

"Thanks for the drinks," said George.


Doug struggled with their bags, tripping once, but maintained his balance. He threw aside the screen door to the cabin, unlocked the door and stepped to one side to allow George and Myrna to go in. The shades to a good-sized window in back of the room were drawn, allowing a flood of sunlight to spill in. The room had wood panelling and screens on the windows. Above the light switch by the door was an eight by ten glossy of Gabby Hayes, his beard well-cared for, looking surprisingly elegant, with just a touch of wistfulness in his eyes.

"I'd shut those windows at night," said Doug. "It can get pretty cold this time of year."

Doug realized suddenly that he was superfluous and left. Myrna waited a few seconds before she pushed on the door to make sure it was firmly closed, then she threw the latch.

She began a detailed survey of the room, going first to the bathroom, leaning into it to see if it was properly cleaned. She walked back to the bed and sat, feet close together, hands primly on her lap.

George, meanwhile, went to the narrow desk above which a mirror was suspended. He turned the straightback chair to face the room and sat, his legs crossed.

"Do you think there's hot water?" she said.

"Of course, there's hot water, Myrna. What do you think?" said George, exasperated.

"You haven't checked, George," said Myrna. "Don't be so certain, not until you check."

George Doskovec threw his arms into the air and went in the bathroom to run the hot water tap. In a few seconds, there was steam rising from the sink bowl.

"There's hot water, Myrna," George said, coming back to sit in the chair. "I'm certain of it, now."

Myrna ignored him. She leaped up from the bed and began to remove her travelling clothes. She laid the jacket out carefully on the bed, smoothing out the sleeves. She then removed the skirt, folded it, and laid it to one side. Her blouse was next. Myrna kicked off her shoes and stood, her back to George, in a full slip that had a lace border on the hem which came half-way up her thighs in a slit. Myrna reached under the slip to remove the smoky-gray pantyhose. As she pulled on the pantyhose, her baggy panties trailed along over her ample buttocks. She tried to extricate them but thought the better of it and removed them as well.

George felt a surge of desire as he watched his wife undressing. Myrna's belly was round and soft, effacing the curve of her hips. Her thighs were a bit heavy as they flowed from her hips.

"Do you want to shower first, or do you want me to," said George.

"I told you to cash in the trip, George," said Myrna. "Bring the large suitcase over here. I might as well unpack."

George brought the suitcase over. He placed it on the bed and snapped it open. His shoulder brushed against Myrna's hair, and he could smell the perfume he'd bought for her birthday.

"I think cash would be better than this. I'm not very impressed. You should have insisted on taking the cash value of the trip, George."

"Myrna, we've gone over it too many times already. There was no way to cash it in. The ticket said you had to take the trip. If the winner couldn't take the trip, they would make another drawing. It would go to someone else. Simple as that," said George, tired of having to explain the same thing over and over again.

"I'd rather it went to someone else, George," she persisted. "I told you to sell it to someone else. Half-price or something. We could have gotten some money out of it and then we wouldn't have to be here."

Myrna's rump was pointed at George as she bent over the suitcase. It was plump and round and it wiggled provocatively. She began to make neat little stacks of their clothes. She was still a handsome woman. Her features were still intact, with just a hint of wrinkles on her temples and at the corners of her mouth. Otherwise, her face was smooth and clear.

George Doskovec looked at his wife with a mixture of familiarity and surprise. Over the years, he had settled into a way of seeing her without seeing her. She was a presence that he could feel even when apart. He drew great comfort from her presence and counted himself among the fortunate for having married her. She could irritate him, she could exasperate him, but he knew there would be little point to living without her.

He reminded himself that there was just a little bit more flesh on her hips this year. The light, energetic body of the young woman he had married was still there, though a little more solid perhaps, but still shapely enough to arouse him and to be the only object of his sexual desire.

"We could enjoy being alone together. We've hardly been alone for many years, now, Myrna," said George. His voice became suddenly hoarse.

Myrna did not answer.

George took his suitcase and set it on the other side of the bed. He opened it and took out his bathrobe. He removed his trousers, folding them, looked in the small closet for a hanger. The pants were draped over his forearm and he held the hanger in his other hand as Myrna came around to the adjacent dresser.

She pulled the second drawer to store her things. From where he stood, watching her stooped over, George saw his wife's ample breasts. The revealed cleavage wobbled carelessly as she moved. George placed the trousers on the hanger, smoothing them to maintain the crease.

George removed his shirt and tie, then his undershirt. He was only slightly overweight, wide in the bottom from the sedentary life he led. He put on the bathrobe and removed his shorts, giving his semi-erect penis a shake.

"What were you saying, George?"

"I said, we're alone. The two of us. We could make this a second honeymoon."

"I wouldn't say we're alone, George. I'd say it's more like we're stranded on a ghost ranch," said Myrna.

"We're not stranded, Myrna, and this is not a ghost ranch," said George, pulling back the counterpane in footlong folds, after which he stacked the pillows vertically against the headboard. He brushed the sheets with the palms of his hands, satisfying himself that they were clean and mildly starched. Before getting in, he tested the firmness of the mattress, hands in a crab position, poking ten fingers as though he were playing the piano.

Myrna finished unpacking, putting away her clothes, complaining about the small number of hangers. She walked to a corner of the bed. Shrugged the straps of her slip from her shoulders to remove her bra.

George reclined on the bed, his legs draped one over the other. George felt himself go stiff as he caught a glimpse of her breasts. He slipped his hand into his bathrobe to play with himself.

"There's just the two of us here, Myrna," said George. "Why don't we take advantage of it."

He massaged his prick until it became rock hard, then he let it go, allowing it to wilt under the bathrobe. George turned on his side to look at Myrna.

"Let's go into Bandera tonight. We'll have something to eat, we'll have some drinks. What do you say?"

"Well, we have to go if we are going to eat tonight, George," Myrna said. She came over to the bed and sat. George moved over to give her some room, draping his arm across her thighs.

"Why don't you take off the rest of your clothes and get in bed with me," he said, inching up her slip to caress her smooth thigh.

"George! It's the middle of the afternoon!" said Myrna, pleasurably surprised.

He slid his hand up along her ribcage to cup her breast. He said, "What of it? We're in the west. We make our own laws. Home rules don't apply."

"You'll fall asleep after, George," said Myrna, giggling, as she draped herself over his chest, snuggling into the crook of his neck, nibbling on the soft flesh beneath and behind his earlobe. "You know you always do, George." She started to fondle him through the bathrobe. "You know you always do," she repeated.


Myrna kissed him lightly on the chin and then laid her head on his chest, feeling through the bathrobe until she found a nipple and then she began to draw little circles around it.

"Is this why you want to be alone?" she purred.

"The thought crossed my mind," said George, enjoying the sweet smell of her hair, running his hand up and down her bottom, enjoying the liquid feel of her slip and the soft pliant flesh under it.

Myrna sighed, slithered a leg over him and pressed her pelvis against his hip. George pulled the slip over her hips, bunching it up at her waist. He brought his hand down, fingers pressed into the cleft of her thighs. He parted her buttocks and poked a finger into her anus. Myrna raised up on her arms and pressed hard into his hips. Her hair fell as a curtain on either side of his face.

"The door's locked," she purred, closing her eyes, her body swelling in a deep sigh.

"Yes, the door's locked," he murmured.

George had his forefinger inside her anus, up to the first joint, feeling her sphincter contract and relax as she gyrated over his hip. Her face above him swooned and became dreamy. Her chin sank into her chest, she pushed her shoulders forward. She purred rhythmically in time to her gyrations.

Myrna stopped suddenly. She jumped off the bed, landed with her feet close together. The slip came over her head, falling where she let go of it. Her loosened breasts were milky and fluid, swaying gently. George, while he watched her, removed his bathrobe.

"Close your eyes, George," said Myrna, leaning over him. She began to kiss his chest, sweeping lightly in a zigzag. She moved over his stomach and onto the soft skin of his lower belly, stopping where his pubic hair began.

George could feel the nipples of her breasts brushing against his hip and thigh. She cupped his testicles, pulling on the loose and wrinkled skin, separating his balls with her thumb. Her hair fell over him, tickling as a light breeze. George arched his hips in arousal and Myrna gripped his prick and squeezed hard, jerking in this direction and that as if she were shifting gears in a transmission.

As soon as George was firm and hard again, she raised her left knee upon the bed and straddled him. Myrna was wet and she felt puffy between her legs. She did not have to guide him in. As she settled down on him, the bulbous head of his penis nestled into the moist declivity. She relaxed the muscles of her thighs and let her full weight drop on him. Instantly, all of him slipped into her body.

The swift insertion pulled a few of her pubic hairs over the fleshy wings of her vagina. She lifted up her bottom an inch or two, to dislodge them. She wiggled her butt until she felt fully comfortable.

Myrna, eyes closed, her hands spread over his chest, leaned all the way back, as far as she could. She clamped her thighs to the sides of his body. She leaned back further, propping herself up with her left hand, while she brought her right hand to the point where she and George were joined. Three of her fingers dug into his pubic hair, while, with her forefinger, she reached for a daub of the viscous moisture she secreted to lubricate the hood of her clitoris. She made circular swipes at it, followed by the application of a long, continuous pressure.

George slid his hands along her thighs, over her hips, lingered briefly at her waist, and then up her ribcage. Myrna's self-ministering had its desired effect. Her clamped knees against George's hips began to throttle in rhythmic, spasmodic jerks. She rocked in a measured rise and fall over him. As George sensed his wife's increasing excitement, he offered himself up with more vigor, matching her movements, pressing his flat hands over her breasts, finding the nipples for his outstretched fingers to cleave to.

Myrna jammed the heel of her hand into her pelvis, making a fist that pressed against herself and which went into the soft part of George's belly. She shuddered quietly as if giving up something against which she had urgently struggled. She raised up her torso so she was perpendicular to George's supine body. Her head dropped, her chin to her chest. And then she came.

Myrna threw her head up in the air suddenly and she raged. Her lips and the skin of chin were pulled down under her gums. Her hands became fists that pummeled her thighs. George felt her body swept up by the gust of her orgasm, seeming to levitate. Released from the constraints of gravity, hovering over him, Myrna's body shook uncontrollably. In a moment or two, she became still, her entire body frozen in an aspect of a painful grimace. She relaxed slightly. The movement made palpable the presence of her husband inside her body. Again she shook uncontrollably.

Myrna collapsed forward on George's chest. She brought her arms around his neck, holding him close. For long minutes, her body shivered again and again as if a sharp, piercing wind swept over her. George withheld his own movements, not daring to move while his wife experienced the recurring throes of her orgasm. Gradually, Myrna became languid, listless, lost in the torpor that came from having exhausted all sensation. George's erection began to subside. Myrna's breathing was long and labored, full of contentment, in his ear.

Myrna's body flowed over George, molding itself to his, as if all of her bones had been sucked away. When she had recovered her senses, she slid over next to him, her head nestled in the crook of his arm. She found George's softening penis where it lay hook-like on his belly. She placed the top of her hand over it and rolled it back and forth trying to straighten out its curvature. It stiffened and she began to stroke it gently, feeling it come to life in her hand. She noticed one of her pubic hairs entangled in the folds of his foreskin. She dislodged it with her thumb without interrupting the flow of her strokes.

George lifted his hips in response and she increased the piston movements of her hand until his entire body became rigid. He directed all of the strength to those of his muscles necessary to his imminent release. She bit into his shoulder, the way he liked it, as the first gob of sperm erupted high over his stomach. George made one spasmodic, uncontrolled sit-up. As the last spasms stopped, Myrna rolled his penis in the goo of his ejaculate. She massaged his belly with the lubricant of his sperm until it dried and left a silky texture to his skin. George tightened his hold on her and gradually let go as he was overcome with sleep.


George and Myrna awoke as the hill country shadows crept inside the Gabby Hayes cabin. A light wind fluttered the spindly branches of the trees outside. George felt stiff and cold. He embraced Myrna for her warmth. His arm was numb from Myrna sleeping on it for the length of their nap. Myrna's mouth was parted, her breathing coming regular and sweet into his face. She felt smooth and soft. He pressed closer to her as he gathered up another erection.

Still drowsy from sleep, George rolled over on top of Myrna. She purred softly, drawing her arms around his neck. Under him, she positioned herself to accept him, reaching between their half-asleep bodies to find and guide him. He entered slowly, trying to savor the sensation of every centimeter of her body sheathing him.

"What's gotten into you, George," Myrna whispered softly into his ear. She sounded hoarse and sluggish from sleep.

Nevertheless, she moved with him, gripping him tightly and pulling down hard on his upstroke. George fucked mechanically, all of his movements concentrated below his waist, his upper torso remaining leaden and heavy over Myrna. In no time, he was pumping so furiously that she could no longer match his movements and simply arched her hips up slightly to better receive his thrusts. George made a grunting sound when he finished. After one final tremor, he rolled over on his back beside her. Myrna smiled, patting him on his stomach.

"Feel better," she asked.

"I feel hungry. Let's go out to eat," said George.

"I'm starved," said Myrna, rising from the bed, shaking her head to clear it, before going to the bathroom. George heard the toilet flush and then he heard the roar of the shower tap. He busied himself unpacking his things from the suitcase, storing them in the top drawer of the bureau. He set aside a change of clothes to go out.

George returned to the bed, where he smoothed out the sheets, fluffed the pillows, rolled back the counterpane. He gathered up the clothes strewn around the bed, disentangling Myrna's panties from the pantyhose. He made a note to himself to ask Ellsworth about laundry service.

Myrna came out of the bathroom wrapped in the towel she'd used to dry herself. Below the edge of towel, a tiny V of her pubic hair sprouted, fluffed and curly. Her hair was wet, plastered to her head. George had placed her suitcase, opened, on the bed.

"God, that was good, George," she said.

"What," George said, distractedly.

"All of it, silly," she said, stopping to kiss him on the forehead.

"Yeah, it was," he said, tweaking her damp pubic hairs.

"Go on," said Myrna, "take a shower. Let's hurry, I'm starved."


An hour later, George and Myrna Doskovec were driving the rattling van into Bandera. Upon leaving Rancho Notorious, George was apprehensive about driving over the limestone road in the dark. He drove slowly and cautiously, squinting into the distance beyond the headlights, trying to see in the dark. Once they were on the blacktop, George relaxed and speeded the van up.

Benjamin Ellsworth had given George directions into town, just to make sure, when George went to pick up the van. He had driven it to the cabin where Myrna waited for him. Ellsworth had also told him that the Basement Saloon was good for dancing.

George parked the van head-in at an angle to the sidewalk. He eased it forward, applying the brakes several times, wanting to stop at the precise point where the tires touched the sidewalk.

"Look, Myrna! That's where they used to tie up horses in the old days," said George, excitedly. "Hitching rails!"

"I never knew you were so interested in the Old West, George. If the whole town makes its living from fake ranches and all those trinkets about cowboys, wouldn't you expect them to put those things up?" Smirked Myrna.

George was saddened that the peaceful interlude at the Gabby Hayes cabin was coming to a close. He hoped Myrna might restrain her constant irritability. Over the years, he had become tolerant of her sudden outbursts and the variability of her moods.

"Did you ever think that those Yankee towns you're so fond of are just as phony?" retorted George, becoming a little irritated himself.

In the aftermath of their lovemaking, there had always been a feeling of warmth and closeness between them, an affirmation of the years they had spent together. These feelings would sustain them until they made love again. As their unions became less frequent, the warmth between them lasted for only brief intervals.

Normally, they'd fall asleep for the night right after making love. He'd drift into consciousness during the night and he'd kiss her hair, or her forehead, grateful that she had married him. In the morning, when the day's obligations took them along separate paths, she spoke to him as she would speak to one of the children.

Myrna was satisfied to make love every two weeks, always in the same way, her on top, assisting herself to an orgasm. In the years during which they'd adopted the routine, it never failed to excite him. George had never wanted another woman.

In between her biweekly cravings, George was satisfied with manual stimulation, two or three times a week, either on his own or with Myrna's participation. It became so difficult to get her to accept him when she wasn't in the mood, that George took to masturbating in the shower or whenever he was sure that Myrna was sound asleep.

She'd caught him at it and instead of being shocked or hurt, she helped him. It was her way of expressing gratitude for George's not insisting that he have her as often as he got the urge. He taught her how to please him. She learned to sense the signals he sent through his body, stroking him to near perfect completion. Depending on how she felt, she'd do him or caress him gently as he finished himself.

Neither of them moved in the van. Myrna kept her silence for a long time. George knew that she was marshaling her reserves to make an overwhelming response. She would deliver it when she was good and ready. He would have preferred to have it out in the van, privately, before going into the restaurant. Myrna threw open the door.

"Let's eat," she said.

"Let's not fight while we're in there, Myrna. Not in front of people," George said.

"I don't think we've ever really had a fight, George," said Myrna.

"Let's not make a scene, then."

"Whatever are you talking about, George," she said, staring at him with a blank face. "I'm hungry. I want to eat. Where do we eat?"

"In there. Right in front of you, Myrna. We'll eat there," said George.

"That man, Mr. Ellsworth, did he say we should eat here? Does it have his recommendation?"

"No, I'm sure it doesn't need his recommendation. Come on, let's go in."

"I don't know, George. You know how I am about restaurants."

"For this once, Myrna. I like the look of this place, to tell you the truth. Let's go in," George said.

"I just don't want us to get into any trouble," said Myrna. "What kind of trouble can we get into in a restaurant? Come on."

"Stop being naive, George. You know perfectly well what I mean. There's bad food, the kind that's unsanitary and poisons you. Or, bugs. You eat a bug mixed up in the food and you get sick. There's unsavory characters, drunks and the like, who like nothing better than trouble. There might be crooks in there who think they can take advantage of us, overcharge, make you pay for things you didn't order. Don't be naive, George. You can get into a lot of trouble in a restaurant."

"If I agree that there is indeed all kinds of trouble to get into in a restaurant, if I were to agree to that, Myrna, can we go in, then? Can we just go in?"

"George," chided Myrna, "you make everything sound like such a big deal."


Inside the restaurant, two men wearing starched white shirts, who had the look of cowboys, were the only customers. To the right as they entered, a waist-high counter stretched the width of the wall. The swivel stools were cut low to the floor. The place was lit by neon beer signs and floodlit beer posters. The restaurant remained dim, taking on an eery atmosphere from the red blue and amber hues of the neon.

George looked at round tables, fat and squat, each surrounded by captain's chairs. George felt the spring in the wooden floor with each step he took and decided he liked the feel of it. He also liked the sharp thud of his heels echoing off the walls.

George and Myrna took a table against the far wall, bringing two chairs close together so they could watch the entrance. As he sat, George caught the eye of one the men sitting nearby. The man nodded a silent greeting. George quickly turned his head away. The cowboys got up, going to the cash register next to the entrance to pay their bill.

George and Myrna asked for the chicken fried steak from the list of house specials scrawled on a framed slate. The order came with cream gravy, mashed potatoes, green beans, and a salad.

"What kind of salad dressing do you have," asked Myrna.

"You name it," said the waitress. "Kraft makes it, we got it."

George ordered a Lone Star beer. The taste of it surprised him but he decided he liked it once he got used to it. Myrna drank a Tab. While they waited for their meal, George Doskovec leaned way back in his chair against the wall as he'd seen movie cowboys do.

Myrna began. "We've never seen as much of New England as we should. See your own backyard first, I always say."

"We've not seen any part of this country, except for New England. And not very much of that," said George.

"People care about the places they're close to, where they have family," Myrna said. "That's what I mean. What do you mean?"

"I mean we should get out more, see more of the country, more places, that's what I mean," said George. "This little town right here is the first place we've ever been to, outside of New England."

"We don't have roots here, George," protested Myrna. "I know where my roots are. I don't think you've ever had roots anywhere."

"What do you mean by that, Myrna?" said George, worried.

"I'm sorry, George. I only mean, your people were immigrants. That's all."

"I'm not ashamed that I came here as an immigrant, Myrna. My father did a lot better than anyone had a right to expect. I haven't done too badly, either. I've doubled the business from what my father left."

"Money isn't everything, George. Family counts," said Myrna.

"Myrna, remember your family reunions?" George said.

"The last one was in Gloucester. Now, that's a pretty town, George. What about it?"

"You're family has reunions all over New England, in places where you don't even have relatives," said George.

"Gloucester is where my part of the family is from. You know that," said Myrna.

"Remember? We flew to Boston, rented a car, and drove there?"

"I don't recall that the drive was noteworthy, George, not for that time of year. What I remember most about Gloucester is special, from when I was a little girl. Memories from when you're little are the best. There's never anything ugly in them.

"Myrna, we've driven all over New England, going through dozens of little towns, lots of them, little towns just like this one. They're old and full of history, and they go begging for people to stop, to look around, to listen. These aren't little girl memories. This is history."

"You're twisting and distorting everything I say, George," said Myrna, petulantly. "Besides, I don't see anything wrong with hurrying to where we're supposed to go."

"Maybe so, Myrna. We have never actually seen the towns is the point I'm trying to make. Myrna, for all we actually know, for all we can actually feel, we've never been any place. We've never struck up a conversation with anyone in any of the places we've been in New England. Does that strike you as odd?"

"Remember that couple we met in Provincetown, the ones who had the little girl who looked so much like a young Liz Taylor? We talked to them!"

"They were Navy people, Myrna, from Newport. They never even told us where they were from. I saw the base decal on the bumper of their car."

"Well, I thought we made a very good impression on them. We could have made friends with them, if we had tried. I think they would have liked it. The little girl was so very pretty and so well-behaved."

"Myrna, you're not even listening to me," said George, exasperated.

"Well, I don't know what's gotten into you, George. I truly have no idea where you are going with this."

"I'll give you an example. Look at the wood in here. On the walls, on the floor. Do you see it?"

"I see it! Quit badgering me," said Myrna. "What's wood got to do with anything. Okay. Fine. I am looking at the wood, George. What is it that you want me to see? I'm waiting, George."

"Maybe, if we'd stopped once, in all those times we drove through New England, maybe, if we'd stopped once to see something. Get involved with it, learn everything there is to know about it."

"What, George, what have we not seen? What do we need to know," asked Myrna. "Stopped to see what? What did we need to see? I don't now what you're getting at."

"It's nothing in particular, Myrna," said George. "It could have been anything. Something. The changing of the leaves. If we had just stopped the car, for once. If we had gotten out of the car. Picked up a leaf from the ground. Studied it. Felt it. Smelled it. If we could have gone into one of the battlefields. Imagined what it was like to fight there. To die there."

"What difference would it make?"

"Everything. A lot. Then, maybe, we'd be better able to appreciate where we are right now. Maybe we'd understand the trouble people go to to make a town like this enjoyable for us."

"I don't think it's so enjoyable, George."

"Skip it," said George.


The waitress brought their meal. She took the order for another beer for George and more water for Myrna.

"Did you ever see a movie called, *Shane*, Myrna," asked George.

"That's an old one, George. Was it about Texas? I saw one called, *Giant*. That one was about Texas. It had Elizabeth Taylor in it. My girl friend and I saw it twice. We saw it one day and then went back again the next day with a big group. All of us went together. It was a long movie, George. Did you ever see it?" said Myrna.

"This place reminds me of Grafton's General Store and Saloon."

"Grafton's?"

"In the movie. It was the hangout for the ranchers who didn't want any farmers in the territory. It was also the only place in the territory for the same farmers to buy supplies. It was built kind of like this. Only, it had beams and rafters all over."

"There are no beams here, George," said Myrna.

"I know. I only said it was kind of built like this. There was sawdust on the floor. I'm just reminded of it, the shape of it, that's all."

"I've never known you to be interested in movie trivia, George," said Myrna. "When I was a little girl, movies were my life. I knew everything there was to know about the movies. I bought a copy of every movie magazine that came out. Come to think of it, I wonder what became of those old magazines. I used to save them, you know. They're probably worth a lot of money today. Mother, I'm sure, threw them out. She'd have no way of knowing, of course, that something like that would someday be worth money."

"*Shane* is a kind of special movie for me. You see, my father never learned to speak English very well. I always suspected he knew a lot more than he let on. When we first came to New York, everybody on our block, everybody we knew, was the same as us. They came over at different times, but we all ended up living in the same neighborhood. Like someone didn't want us spread out all over. That's why I never felt as though I was in a foreign country. There was this abandoned building where refugees like us had meetings. It was on the same block where my father had his shop. We cleaned it and painted it. Sometimes—this was the best part—they would show a movie. An old one, from before the war. We had to wait until after dark because of the big windows from when the building was a store or something. They were too big for drapes. They would start the projector and we would see our homeland, the way it was. In the movie, there would be songs and laughter and the people on the screen talked in our language. It never failed. Every time they showed one of those movies, my father and everybody around him would end up with tears in their eyes. They weren't sad movies. The memories they brought were so painful for everyone that they ended up crying anyway. For days after the showing of one of those movies, my father would drink in the kitchen of the small apartment where we lived. He wouldn't get drunk, not to where he fell down or bumped into things. He would just drink and drink, not saying a word to anybody, and after a long time, he would start crying. He wouldn't make a sound. His cheeks would be wet, but he didn't wipe them. Then he would put away the bottle and go to bed. The whole time he never said a word to anybody."

"He was homesick, George," said Myrna.

"I think it was more than homesick, Myrna. I was still fairly young when we came here. I hardly even remember living in the old country. The move didn't make that much of an impression on me. For my father, the thought of never seeing his homeland again was more than he could keep inside him sometimes."

"Couldn't he go back and visit? He made enough money to travel.

When he retired, he could've gone back, couldn't he?"

"No, we were seen as traitors by our relatives who stayed behind. The country had to be rebuilt after the war. They saw my father and the others as people who turned their backs on their duty and fled. Traitors," said George.

"What about later, after the country was on its feet again? Surely, they wouldn't carry a grudge over something like that."

"My father wrote to his relatives but they never answered. They were partisans, real patriots. My father's leaving hit them worse than some others. They were national heroes and they felt disgraced by my father. Our neighbors in those first years, my father stayed in touch with them until he died, they got a chance to go back. He thought that maybe with his success they'd soften their hearts toward us. Instead of better, things became worse. The country became Communist after the war. My father's family joined the Communist Party and they were ashamed that one of their relatives had become a rich capitalist. I felt sad for my father everytime he saw one of those old movies from the homeland. I wanted him to see a movie that was different, maybe one where he might enjoy himself. When I got my idea, *Shane* was playing on Times Square. I made him bring me all the way out to Times Square to see it. It was the first American movie we saw together."

"Did he like it," asked Myrna.

"I don't know. He never said. I was afraid I had offended him because he never mentioned it once. I never asked him to take me out to another movie."


They finished their meal. The waitress cleared away the table. Myrna commented that she couldn't see what the big deal was with chicken fried steaks. George paid the bill and they walked outside into the cool evening. George Doskovec hitched up his trousers and twiddled a toothpick in his mouth. They stopped a few feet away from the van. George stood on the edge of the sidewalk, looking up and down the street.

"You know what I feel like right now, Myrna? I feel like Jack Palance. He was the outlaw that was brought in to do away with the farmers who wouldn't give up their land. He's the one that Shane has to kill in order to make the territory safe. Jack Palance wore a black leather vest and two six-guns. Every time he was going to kill somebody, he grinned like the devil and he put a black glove on his gunhand. That was the signal that somebody was going to die."

"I don't understand you, George. You say, you feel like a killer in a movie."

"No, Myrna. Not a killer. That's not it at all. It's just that, for a second back there, when we came out of the restaurant, I remembered the image of Jack Palance stepping out of Grafton's Saloon. Tall and confident, like he'd faced death many times and he was invincible. I could feel, at that instant, what it must be like to be on your own, without the law to protect you.

"I don't get it, George," said Myrna.

"Well, look at the street, Myrna. There's not a soul to be seen. Look up at the sky, see how clear and clean it is. We're the only people standing in all of the street here. I noticed it right away. I could actually feel it, what it was like in the Old West. What it was that brought people out here in the first place. A little town like this might be the only civilization for a hundred miles in any given direction. That's why Jack Palance had to die in the movie. The farmers were bringing community justice, you know, the common good over the individual. The safety of numbers, cattle huddled together in a herd. Along with it, they'd bring civilization, modern life, unbounded faith in the future. Jack Palance had that unrestrained spark that we all carry, the will to throw your freedom in people's faces. Shane, Alan Ladd, had that same spark. Jack Palance was trying to keep this a country of free individuals, even if it meant killing all the farmers. Shane, Alan Ladd, knew that unrestrained freedom is destructive to a civilized community. Once he kills Jack Palace, he knows that he, too, will be destroyed in the end. He knew enough to remove himself before he became dangerous. Jack Palance was pure to the end. What I felt, back there, is that same spark of unrestrained freedom. As quickly as I felt it, at almost the exact same instant, I became on guard against it. People who enjoy complete freedom either destroy themselves or become destroyed. Automatically, just as the spark of Jack Palance flashed through me, I suppressed it. I didn't even have to think about it."

"Oh, let's go back, George," said Myrna. "I want to go to bed again."

# The Little Tin Sailor

My father said, "Not in the long run, it don't mean nothin'. Not in the long run."

I had finished telling him that my mother was suing him for divorce.

"So she wants to end it, hunh? Is that what brought you out here?" he said.

I was surprised by the bitterness that underlay the sarcasm in the remark. He had not lived with my mother for more than thirty years. A divorce would make formal the separate lives they had lived. I didn't think he'd be too upset by it.

"It's usually pretty hard to get in touch with you," I said. "I don't see you unless you find me first. You don't want to be found, nobody finds you," I said hoping I didn't sound too critical.

"What the fuck is that supposed to mean? You're turning into some kind of fucking wiseguy, or something? Fucking wiseguy!"

"No, sir. In the time you've lived here, you've had four addresses and six different telephone numbers. I called you where you lived before, the phone was disconnected. I just happened to remember the name of the apartment complex and I called the office and they said you were gone, you didn't leave a forwarding address. So, I wait, I waited. I sent you two letters thinking the post office would get them to you. Maybe you got them, maybe not. You never answered."

"Goddamned right, I didn't answer. You don't know shit, do you, wiseguy? I want to talk to you, I call you. That's all you have to know. Ain't that right, wiseguy?"

"That's the way it's been, sir."

"Goddamned right!"

I sat in my father's apartment, on a long imitation-leather couch. He had been standing inside the kitchen facing me through an opening in the wall, elbows resting on a chest-high bar. The couch faced away from him. All the while, I'd had to twist my neck to look at him. He'd tossed back a tumbler-full of tomato juice and vodka, after which he had poured four fingers of straight vodka into another glass.

He came out into the living room area, shoulders thrown back. He began to pace back and forth in the narrow space between the loveseat facing me and a coffeetable. His facial muscles twitched, there was slobber at the corner of his mouth. He waved his arms and he moved his head as if he were listening to and agreeing with something he said inside himself. He swayed from side to side as if he were anticipating the pitch and roll of a ship at sea.

He waved his drink in the air as he gestured. Each time he did so he came perilously close to spilling the drink. Yet, he maintained an awkward balance that came from the many years he had spent at sea on the decks of Navy ships.

I'd always had an image of my father, tall in his dress blues, Dixiecup hat tilted to one side, resting his hands on the spokes of the helm. He would be standing tall and steady as the ship pitched and rolled. Others on the bridge would be hurled all about, but not him, not my father.

Each time I had met him, he had seemed a different man. Our meetings were spaced at long intervals over the years. It occurred to me that my father was not so much different, perhaps, but that as it happened each time I saw him I noticed different things about him. For instance in this meeting I noticed the boozey paunch and the stooped shoulders that made him seem shorter than he was. It was obvious to me that a paunch is necessary to a life-long drinking man. I couldn't be sure, though, if he'd had that paunch the last time I had seen him.

Even in the mothball fleet, as he called his retirement, he kept his hair clipped military short. His hair was gray, like the painted warships he'd served on. His nose was misshapen from a fistfight or two, bulbous, with flecks of flared veins. It was a boozer's nose. The belled cuffs of his polyester trousers were a cruel joke on his Navy career.

My father calmed down a little. He sat on the loveseat, leaning forward, elbows on his knees. He sipped his drink and looked at me. Deep, bulky furrows formed on his forehead.

"Not in the long run, it don't mean nothin'," he said, lowering his head to peer into the contents of the glass. He saw something in it. He snorted and took another drink. "Not in the long run."


The earliest memory I had of anything having to do with my father was not of himself in the flesh, but rather of a box wrapped in brown paper, bound with baling twine. My mother said the box came from far away, across half the world and over on the other side of the Pacific Ocean. It came from a place called the Philippines. In my mind, the ocean I managed to conjure up was no bigger and no more troublesome than the lake where my grandfather took me fishing.

It was a few weeks before Christmas. The weather was unusually cold for San Antonio. I had spent the morning knocking off icicles from the trees in the back yard. My sister and I were playing inside the house when there was a knock on our door.

At first, we thought it was a tree branch or something banging against the house. It was too cold for anyone to be outside. But then the knock came again, more forcefully, breaking into the quiet warmth of our living room. We became afraid, wondering what it could be. No one ever knocked on our door. Our neighbors and my playmates usually walked in, as my mother always kept the door unlocked.

My mother went to open the door and when she did a draft of thick wintry air slithered in just above the floor, sweeping over my sister and me like a cold blanket. I shivered and my sister hugged herself, giggling, tickled by the fluttering wind.

The postman wore a uniform like a policeman and for a moment I thought he would take my mother away. My sister sensed my fear and upon seeing the uniform, she stopped her giggling and she began to cry. I brought my finger up to my lips and shushed her. Her eyes opened wide in anticipation.

"It's presents from your father," said my mother, turning and closing the door behind her. "I bet he got them from Santa Claus."

"Daddy knows Santa Claus!" yelped my sister, clapping her hands in glee.

All I could actually see was a box wrapped in brown paper. My mother went to her sewing box where she got a pair of scissors. She sat down on the floor with my sister and me, near the space heater in the corner. There was a Christmas tree, two feet in height on the endtable.

It took my mother the longest time to unwrap the box. It was crushed in several places. She lifted the folded edges of the paper, smoothed out the wrapping, cutting carefully through the cellophane tape. Beneath the brown paper was another layer of wrapping paper, this one a glossy royal blue, held together by strips of red ribbon. My sister and I were impatient, urging my mother to hurry.

She went about it slowly, holding up a piece of ribbon and asking us what to do next, teasing my sister and me until we screamed our impatience, begging her to hurry and get to the contents. Finally, she unwrapped the box.

Then she stopped altogether and asked if it might not be better to wait until Christmas. She told us it would be fun were we to imagine what it could be that my father sent. She said we could make a game of it, making a wish every day, hoping what we wished for was in the box.

Best of all would be Christmas morning when we'd find out what wish got granted. My sister, who had just begun to talk, wished for candy. I didn't want to play.

My mother's Christmas presents hadn't been any fun, at least, not until after she started to work. She made sure we got what we needed and there wasn't anything left for presents a kid would like. A pair of pants, shirts, socks, that sort of thing. I was old enough to understand what a Christmas without a father meant.

When the box of gifts came, I think she still believed in their marriage. She was convinced that one day my father would come back and we would all be together. My grandfather had given her some money, making her promise to buy us presents. Instead, she'd used it to buy clothes for us. She did promise to make a nice dinner, something special, and that was all that we looked forward to on Christmas day. Until, that is, the box from my father came. There we were, eager and about to crawl out of our skins, and my mother wanted to play games.

My mother stopped teasing and opened the box.

The first object was wrapped in tissue paper, bound with a rubberband. My name was written on a slip of paper tucked under the rubberband. It turned out to be a tin sailor, dressed in a tar blouse of blue with the flap in back permanently windswept, frozen. In the front was a painted neckerchief of red and white wide stripes. On the bib of the blouse was a square with rounded corners set off by dots of yellow paint that were meant to be buttons. On the sailor's head was a black tam-o'-shanter with a tin tassel painted red.

The sailor's leg had been crushed somewhere during its long journey. My mother held it up for me to inspect, turning it around, saying that it was a sailor in uniform, which I already was old enough to know. She reminded my sister and me that our father was a sailor. I knew that, too. I kept my eyes on the crushed leg. My mother extended it for me to hold, but I refused to touch it.

My mother was resourceful. Before trying to give it to me again, she removed the sailor's foot from the metal tube that formed the leg. With the scissors shoved inside the tube, she tried as best she could to smooth it out by turning it round and round. In the end, the flattened leg became somewhat round, albeit creased, with several chippings in the paint.

It was enough, though, to give the leg a semblance of normalcy. After she had replaced the foot to the leg, my mother handed the tin sailor to me. At that moment, I put the flaw out of my head and it became my favorite possession. I wrapped it in a piece of cloth and stored it at the bottom of a box of toys. I'd take it out once in a while to look at it.

In later years, I lost all interest in the little tin sailor. My mother had given up all hope of ever restoring our family. One day, I discovered that my mother had taken my little tin sailor and had placed it next to a photograph of my father that she kept in her room.


In all the time I was growing up, my father had never come to visit us. He had seen me, according to my mother, when I was a few months old, but he had not seen me since and he had never seen my sister at all. All we had of him was a blurry photograph in which he smiled because he was happy and because he was young and because there was so much he didn't know.

The airbrushed coloring on his cheeks and forehead and the glare from the oval picture frame made him look as if he had always been a memory. There was an ethereal quality to the pose, as if he knew at the moment that he posed for the picture that it would be all that we would ever have of him. I told my mother once that in the picture, it looked like my father wore lipstick. My mother laughed and told me not to be disrespectful.

As my sister and I became older, went to school, and had a constant and pressing need for money, my mother went to work. My father had sent money from the very beginning, but as time went on, he sent less of it less often. There were times when I would see my mother crying, wondering what would become of us. Sometimes, she and my grandfather would go into her room, closing the door. From the living room, I could hear them arguing. I knew they argued about my father. Once she was working, my mother never cried again, at least not where I saw her. Times sure became happier for us.

In all the time we were growing up, my mother never said a nasty or unkind thing about my father. We were expected to be polite and reverent when we mentioned him. It was like talking about a dead person. My sister and I were occasionally curious about his absolute absence from our lives. Other kids had fathers who came home every night. There was one family where the father came to visit only on weekends, but at least they saw him. My mother would only say that my father was away at sea and that it wasn't easy for him to get away. That was all we knew about my father, that he was always away at sea. In time, we came to understand the fiction and stopped asking to know more.

I did not have any feelings at all about my father. He was a ghostly face in a tinted photograph who had sent to me a little tin sailor with a crushed leg. I did not know anything else about him and I never imagined that one day I would meet him. Consequently, I never grew up wondering what I would say to him when we met. When the time came to meet him, there was little I could do to prepare. I was horrified, that's all.

My sister, on the other hand, hated him. It's hard to say just when she began to feel that way. We first knew of it when my sister threw a jar of hand lotion at the picture of my father that my mother kept on top of her dresser. She broke the glass in the frame and scratched a little the glossy surface of the tinted photograph. I was waiting for my mother to spank the hell out of her. Instead, she got another frame, restored the picture, and it was like the incident never happened. It was never mentioned again but we knew that my sister had an intense, bitter hatred toward him.


My mother read a letter to us in which my father asked if I would care to meet with him during my senior class trip to San Francisco. His ship was going through pierside repairs in Oakland after riding out a typhoon. It wouldn't be any problem, he said, to shoot on over the bridge for a visit.

"No, you mustn't see him. You just can't," my sister screamed. "He can't come into our lives, not after not giving a damn about us, ever!"

If I agreed to see my father, I would betray the family. Ever since my grandfather had died, it had been just the three of us. My sister insisted that we not even talk about it. She stormed out of the room when my mother and I didn't agree with her immediately.

With my sister out of the way, my mother explained to me that she had written to my father about my high school graduation and about the trip to San Francisco. It was the first I knew with certainty that she wrote to him and he to her. There were letters I'd seen which I suspected were from him. I'd see my mother reading a stack of them from time to time. She never let on. I kept what I'd seen to myself.

She handed me a money order for fifty dollars. It had come with the letter, she said. Even if I refused to meet him, I could keep it. I took it in my hands and held it for a while. I shook my head and told her I couldn't keep it, that rightfully, it belonged to her. She knew I meant it, too. She smiled, touched me on the cheek, and said she'd deposit it in my college account.

My sister, who had retreated to her room, but who had kept the door ajar so she could listen, came back.

"Please don't," she said, and went quietly back to her room again.

My mother asked me what I wanted to do. I told her, honestly, that I didn't know. I asked her what she thought I should do. She always had good advice for me. I never knew my mother to hesitate or equivocate when a decision was called for. She said I should go on and meet with him.

"How come?" I said.

"It is time," she said.


"I'd recognize you anywhere," said my father.

The best I could come up with was a handshake and my father seemed satisfied with that. I avoided looking into his face as much as was possible without being impolite.

"What say we go over to the coffeeshop. Bar's no place for a scholar and a gentleman," he said.

The light was much better in the coffeeshop. I took a good look at him and he took a good look at me. The face in the tinted picture, indelible in my mind, was nothing more than a boy no older than I, a stranger, really, compared to the man who sat across the table from me.

In fact, I probably had expected a flesh and blood version of the face captured in the photograph. It was not to be, of course. Instead, he was thin, with just the first showings of his beer belly. His face was oddly jowly and loose. He wore the ill-fitting, seldom used, civilian clothes of sailors on liberty.

I had nothing much to say to him and he had nothing much to say to me. There wasn't very much that we had in common. Except his blood, and there's not much conversation in that.

He asked about school. He did so in a way that told me he was not too interested in what I had to tell him. It was a way to fill up the silence between us. Or, perhaps if he could get me talking, he wouldn't have to worry about what I was thinking.

I thought he would be proud of the four college scholarship offers I had received. I mentioned the one I had finally accepted and then told him it presented the best chance for me to go on to law school. I waited for him to be impressed.

Instead, he seemed impatient to have his turn to impress me. He told me he had been assigned to a duty station on the east coast. Shore duty. Lifers, he said, give a left nut for shore duty. He didn't want it. He said it wasn't right that the Navy would trip him up like that. He was a West Coast sailor and all he ever asked of the Navy was to stay on the West Coast.

I told him I was facing at least seven years of college, then another year after law school to study for the bar. In reply, he said he was on his last tour before finishing his twenty. I told him we, my class, were scheduled to attend a symphony performance that night. He was seriously thinking of shipping over and staying in for thirty. He said there wasn't much a guy like him could do. The Navy was his home. He looked at me kind of funny when he said that. I looked away.

Not once did he ask about my mother or my sister.


As we struggled for conversation, he kept drinking beers. They brought them in from the bar for him, one right after the other. He drank them so fast that he kept the waitress busy just with our table. Each time he ordered another beer, he would ask me if I wanted one. I stayed with sodas.

Through the window of the coffeeshop that gave out to the street, I saw a girl, an Oriental, not too much older than I, who was pacing up and down the hill. When she got to the window, she would look at my father and me, turn, and walk downhill again. A few minutes later, she'd be back, glare into the window and go on.

Finally, after pacing back and forth for about fifteen minutes, with great impatience, she came inside. She walked right up to my father. He looked at her, frowned, but he moved over so she could sit down beside him.

"You said you'd be just a little while, didn't you?" said the girl, annoyed and pouting. "It's more than a little while."

"It's my son," said my father, helplessly. "Meet my son."

The girl didn't even bother to look at me.

"Come on," she whined. "We have to go, or I'm going to be late for work. You promised me. I'm not going to let you break your promise!"

My father gave me a 'you-know-how-it-is' kind of look. He turned his hands palm side up. He told the girl to go on, to wait for him outside. He had to pay the check. She shot him a look distinguished by her compressed bloodless lips. She obeyed, though, and left us to our last few seconds together.

"Listen," my father said, uncomfortably, "your mother, she doesn't have to know about the girl, o.k.? You never saw the girl. It's not right she should know something like that, your mother. You understand, don't you? Besides, it's nothing anyway. I ship out, it's over. Got it?"

He reached in his pocket for a wad of bills. They were pinned together by a money clip in the shape of a dragon.

"Kid like you," he said, "high school, you always need some cash, right?"

He pulled out three twenties. He arched an eyebrow at me, as if asking if it were enough.

"Aw, hell," he said, and then pulled out two more. "Take your girl out. You got a girl, don't you? Treat your buddies, or something. Tell them it's on your old man, right!"

He gave the hundred dollars to me.

"Listen, I have to go," he said. "I hope you understand how it is, kid."

I felt, right then, just as our visit was over, that there was much more he could say to me and I to him. Even as he prepared to leave, I could have kicked myself in the pants, thinking that there had to be more to it. There was a lot more he could have said about himself to make me know and understand him a little. I too could have said a lot more. I didn't know how to try. Instead, we just looked at each other for a final few seconds.

"Pay the bill, will you?" he said.

Watching him leave the coffeeshop, I noticed how he walked with his shoulders thrust back. His torso swayed from side to side as if he were still on the deck of a ship.

Back home, neither my mother nor my sister mentioned my meeting with him. I didn't expect them to cross-examine me for details, but I did expect more curiosity than they displayed. I was determined not to bring the subject up on my own. I was soon busy with preparations to go away for college and I stored away the memory of that first meeting with my father.


The next time I saw my father, it was six years later. The place this time was Washington, D.C. When he called, I agreed to meet him without hesitation. There was no need for a family discussion as to whether I ought meet him because I was on my own by then. And, I was curious about him.

I was going to law school in New York when he called. He said he had finished two tours of shore duty and had been transferred to a ship homeported in Norfolk. He had a long weekend liberty coming up and he thought he'd spend it in the City. He called it "the City". He asked if I would have a drink with him.

There was a group of us going to Washington to protest the government's policies in support of Somoza. I'd be away all weekend. It would have to be another time. He made a quick change of plans, right on the telephone, and said, maybe a weekend in DC wouldn't be so bad. He gave me the name of a hotel where he would stay. We ended the conversation with him saying, if you get a chance, give me a call.

My participation in the protest amounted to no more than serving as a body to swell the ranks, fill in the sea of faces for the television cameras.

Janice, my fiancee, was intense and committed to changing the world for the better. As one of the organizers, she was going to be extremely busy. She would appreciate it if I didn't hang around so much. She'd tell me, without giving a thought as to whether she might hurt my feelings, that I made her nervous, loitering as I did with nothing to do. I could easily get away for an hour or two.

In our last meeting in San Francisco, I had been on the threshold of manhood; more child than man. I had gone to the meeting with the hope of finding my father. Instead, I had found someone who was not particularly interested in being a father, anybody's father.

For many months afterward, I thought about him more than I ever had in my life. I was trying to come to terms with what makes a man abandon his family altogether. In thinking about him, although I had very little to work with, I had come to feel that I understood a little about him. It was nothing more than homemade psychology on my part, but it seemed to fit my father. It was always difficult for me to express my feelings. I worried that deep down I might feel about him as my sister did.

In the aftermath of that first meeting, I experienced contrary feelings of anger, pain and confusion. I could not bring myself to discuss it either with my mother or my sister. In time, as the pain lessened, I understood a little more about myself. I began to hope that someday things would change, that he and I would someday embrace one another as father and son.


When we met in Washington, it was still difficult for us to say things to each other. I thought that part of it, at least, would be different. There was a barrier between us that neither of us could find the words to overcome. To fill in the silences that settled in after brief, truncated exchanges of conversation, my father flirted with the waitress.

She seemed to be about my age. She wore a black maid's outfit, trimmed in white. The skirt of it was not long enough to cover her buttocks which were covered in white ruffled underpants. Black stockings, with a red garter on her right thigh, completed the outfit.

Each time she brought him a drink, my father would say under his breath, "Juicy!"

The bar was full of men who appeared to be either businessmen or civil servants. I wore a jacket and tie, a habit I had acquired upon beginning law school. My father wore a windbreaker and jeans. The chairs in the bar were low to the floor and they swivelled.

The waitress had taken a definite liking to my father. Each time she came to our table, she purposely bent low as she placed his drink in front of him so he could get a good look at her breasts.

While he scanned the room to ogle the waitress, he asked if I had ever thought about joining the Navy. The truth is, it had never even occurred to me. He told me I could have a cush berth as an officer, good chow, waited on hand and foot by the filipino stewards.

It'd be better if I went in as a lawyer, he went on, with the Judge Advocate. Aircraft carriers and shore duty is about all I could expect for assignments. Maybe overseas, in Spain, or the Philippines. Not too shabby for duty stations. I made it clear to him that the Navy was not in my future. He shrugged and said I could do worse. The Navy had done fine by him.

I told him a little about my sister, how she'd gotten married. How she'd had a little girl. I asked how he felt to be a grandfather. He frowned, upending his drink and draining it. He held his arm up for the waitress. I thought my lame attempt at levity had not gone over too well.

He asked me if I knew that he had tried to visit my sister. Meet somewhere with her. Of course, I had not been told. Ever since my first meeting with my father, the subject had become a sore point between us. He told me my sister did not care for him at all.

Shortly after she got married, he had offered to fly her and her husband anywhere in the country, pay for everything. It'd be like a honeymoon for them, all expenses paid. If she would just meet with him for a little bit. So he could see what she looked like.

She had not bothered to answer him. He had written once more but the letter was returned undelivered. My mother, he said, would do nothing to help. I think he expected that she would. There was nothing in the way he told it that indicated he wanted my help.

"She probably hates me," he said. He tried to sound as if he weren't botherered, either way, by it.

"Have you ever thought of going to San Antonio yourself?" I asked. "If you were in town and called, she might see you."

"Think that'll work?" he asked.

"No," I said.

"Then, what the fuck you getting at?" He wasn't angry. He wanted to end the subject, go on to something else.

"If you were around, kept your distance, but you let it be known you're around, things might change. You never know. People change as they get older," I said.

"No, not that. Not yet. I can't go back," he said.

We were quiet while he ordered another drink. When the waitress brought it, she lingered at the table. He put his hand on her hip and she seemed to edge a little closer to him. She asked what he had in mind. He told her they'd have to talk about it. Whenever, she said.

He began to ask me questions about my mother. He was curious, genuinely so it seemed, but he asked about things I had no way of knowing. He asked if she was sleeping with anyone, which left me stunned when he asked. My mother had never gone out with any man the whole time I lived at home. It would be very unlikely that she would take up with someone since I'd left. In any case, it was something I would consider an extremely private matter for her. Not any of my business and certainly, not any of my father's.

"I don't know," I said.

"Little shit," he said. "You wouldn't tell me if you knew, would you? The way I figure it, you don't know. It could be happening right under your fucking nose the whole fucking time and you wouldn't fucking know, would you? Mommy's not supposed to do stuff like that. I want you to know, you can tell her if you want, I would understand something like that."

He finished his little speech and got busy grinning at the waitress. It would be a while before he got back to me. I had a moment to think over some things.

I had spent four years in school in Austin, coming back to visit every month or so. I stayed with her during the summer vacations when I had to work. She'd done pretty well with her job. Over the years, she'd put away enough to help out on things that my scholarship did not cover. Of course, I wanted a stereo one year and I had to work for it. My sophomore year, she bought a car for me. For the next two summers, I worked to help her pay for it.

She'd bought a house for us just before I started in high school. She wanted us to live in a nicer neighborhood so my sister and I could attend a better school. While I was away at school, she kept my room unchanged. I began to notice more and more that I didn't belong there anymore. That I was coming back to something that was no longer mine. It was something that I was beginning to feel within myself. It made me sad, and it worried me. What I felt, what I was looking into, was a future where I would be alone.

In that crucial period of transition, my passage to an initially bewildered manhood, I felt that I had gone farther than I intended. I felt adrift in a sandstorm, with no sense of direction. I had a sense of moving, motion for its own sake. It was not until I met Janice that things cleared up for me.

In the process, I became conscious of my mother as a human being. I began to respect her privacy. If there were things about my mother that she did not share with my sister and me, it dawned on me during this period that it was not important for me to know everything she did.

My sense of my mother did not rely on things I knew about her. Concrete, observable, things. My sense of her, rather, was based on feelings that I had toward her, begun even before I was born. I wondered, as my thoughts came back to my father, if, had he been at home all the while, would I have had the same sense about him.

The questions that my father had for me about her were not only intrusive of her privacy but called for intimate details that I did not know. I had the feeling that he did not particularly want to know either. He was testing me.

There were things I could tell him about my mother, if he'd quit ogling the waitress. How pleased she was whenever my sister or I had dinner waiting for her when she came home from work. Or, the pride she took in my getting a lead role in my high school production of *Inherit the Wind*. How I caught her crying in the hospital corridor when my little niece was born. I could tell him hundreds of things like that. In fact, I had a lifetime of things like that to tell him.

The waitress was at her station by the bar. She'd crossed her arms on the bar, rested her chin on them. She kept smiling at my father. He blew a kiss at her and she laughed. He downed his drink quickly and raised the empty glass.

As a signal that our meeting was at an end, my father asked if I needed money.

"You're a fucking student, right?" he said. "Students never have any fucking money."

"I'm alright," I said, a little embarrassed. "I don't need any money."

I expected that he was going to force the money on me as he took out his wallet. Instead, he took out some bills and handed them to the waitress. He told her to take out for the drinks and to keep the change. Their hands touched and held for a moment before she went back to the bar.

We shook hands. He promised to keep in touch, although not altogether sincerely.

"I mean it this time," he said.

He spoke in a way that told me there were other things on his mind. As he walked to the exit that gave into the hotel lobby, the waitress was standing there, smoking a cigarette. She was waiting for him. He took her by the arm and spoke a few words to her. She threw her head back and laughed.

I very badly wanted to be with Janice. I left them standing with their heads bent, foreheads almost touching, as I walked out of the bar.

I landed with a nice firm in New York right after law school. Janice and I graduated in the same class. She accepted a position consistent with her determination to change the world for the better.

We set up an apartment together. I wanted an apartment in a nice neighborhood, I could afford it, after all. Janice wanted to live in Harlem. We compromised with a nice place in Chinatown, a few blocks off Canal.

In no time at all, it seems, we became settled and comfortable. We passed the bar and I began to receive my promotions on schedule. Janice grew more and more frustrated as the new administration in Washington began to dismantle, in seemingly innocuous and piecemeal ways, the entire civil rights apparatus that took twenty-five years to construct.

Initially, she had been excited at the prospect of winning new battles. It was a way of leaving her mark, as it were, on the social fabric of the nation. She found herself fighting legal battles previously won. With the Justice Department now in opposition, Janice and her colleagues were beleaguered and at the end of their rope. After five years, Janice was exhausted and our relationship was in trouble.

On the day Ed Meese was sworn in as Attorney General, Janice moved out of our apartment. We agreed that she needed some time by herself, which she decided to spend in a little place she found in the Bronx.

We continued to see each other exclusively. We spent our evenings and weekends together, so the separation was not difficult to bear. Janice's boss asked her to quit, for her own good. She'd given more than anyone had a right to expect. It was time for her to move on. Put her life together.

With a loan from her parents, she went to Europe, where she stayed for three months. I caught up with her in Norway, in a little town outside of Oslo. She'd taken rooms with a dairy farmer and his wife. They were very taken with Janice. We spent a week together before I convinced her that we should settle down and marry.

We were married in Paducah, Kentucky. My mother and sister came up from San Antonio for the wedding. Janice's mother managed the large and noisy affair, which was a considerable undertaking. Janice had obviously alerted her folks and thus the subject of my father never came up. My mother and sister, of course, charmed every one of Janice's relatives.

Janice and I had gone to visit my mother, on holidays and such, over the whole time we had been together. Each time, we stayed in my old room, still unchanged, and which Janice adored. If my mother had reservations about Janice and I not being married and sleeping together during those visits, she never let on. She was very pleased that

Janice was in love with me.

It was therefore surprising to her, when Janice and I arrived in San Antonio for our honeymoon, that we chose to stay at a downtown hotel. Janice and I needed the privacy. There was no doubt that marriage was right for us. Everything else, though, was not so certain. We still had a long way to go in determining the shape our lives would take.

We spent endless hours on the balcony of our hotel room overlooking the Riverwalk. By the time our honeymoon was over, we had decided to live in San Antonio. It was a nice choice of a place to raise kids. I would resign from the firm in New York and find something in San Antonio. Janice would have a baby right away, stay home, and when the time was right, she would begin to practice law again.

The plans Janice and I made for our lives were not too difficult to fulfill. I got on with a local firm, at a salary one-third less than what I was paid in New York. For San Antonio, it was generous, indeed.

Janice shopped around for a job, but found nothing that was even remotely interesting. Instead of despairing, she opened up her own law practice. Through a couple of cases which brought her considerable television exposure, she quickly became the queen counsel of drug peddlers, earning twice what I made.


We had been in San Antonio something like three years, when my secretary took a telephone call from someone who insisted he would speak only with me. He had refused to identify himself or even say what he wanted. My secretary asked if I wanted to take the call. I recognized the voice instantly. I almost said, 'dad,' but in the end I caught myself and simply called him, 'sir.' He said I shouldn't call him 'sir' because he had never been an officer. In fact, he said, he was out of that canoe club, the Navy, for good. I was already developing an impatience with trivial things and waited for him to tell me what the call was about. I knew he wasn't calling to tell me he had retired. My father had put in his thirty years in the Navy and he had, as he put it, bailed out two years before. He had been living in San Antonio the whole time. I was surprised. I told him that I had been back in town myself for a little longer than that. "Yeah, I know," he said, and let it go at that. I was busy working on something and was impatient to return to it. To end the conversation, I invited him over to the house for dinner. I told him he could meet my wife and two sons.

"You did what!" screeched my sister. I felt it was important that they know I had invited my father over for dinner. We were gathered at my mother's. Since returning home, Janice and I ate Sunday dinner at my mother's every month or so. The dinners were usually quiet and pleasant, in spite of our two children and my sister's three. The subject of my father seldom came up in our conversations. Especially, the subject never came up in front of my sister. If anything, her outbursts had become even more virulent over the years. Janice knew what was coming. She took the children out to the backyard to play. I wanted to wait until we were alone, to spare the children. Janice had exempted herself from the start. My mother's reaction told me that she knew about it already. "What's he doing here?" my sister wanted to know. "He doesn't belong here! Why did he have to come back? What does he want?"

"He's retired from the Navy. He's been living here for a while," I said. "He hadn't called me before. A couple of days ago is the first I knew he was here."

"I've talked to him," said my mother, "he calls every day. He even wants to see me."

"What's he want? I know he wants something," said my sister. "Me. That's what he says, at least. He says he wants to start over again. According to him, he wants to make things right," said my mother, through a haze of smoke. She'd taken up smoking shortly after she retired from her job. "He hasn't seen you in thirty goddamned years!" hissed my sister. "Let's keep this civilized, how about it?" I said. My sister ignored me. "He thinks he can just come back and it's like nothing ever happened. What about all those years? What about what he did to us? Doesn't that count for something. It's not fair, it's just not fair!"

"What's not fair," asked my mother, confused. "You're getting hysterical. What's this about fairness?" I said. My sister got up from the table. She crossed her arms and began to walk around my mother and me. Hovering, glaring. I kept my head lowered, my fingers laced in front of me. My mother distracted herself with her cigarette. Over the years, she had gotten into the habit of distancing herself during my sister's outbursts. "You've never been one much for romance," laughed my mother, at last. "Mom, I wish you would be serious. This is very important!" said my sister, coming back to her chair. The walk around the table had done some good. She was calm, ready to talk. "Serious?" said my mother. "Of course, I'm serious. I grew up being in love with your father. We were children in love. Fifteen, or sixteen. At seventeen, we got married. It was the most natural thing to do. We were married and lived alone. Away from his folks and mine. Neither of us had ever been happier. We thought it would last forever. We were children in love. He couldn't find steady work. He'd work a day here and a day there. We didn't mind too much because it meant that we had more time to be together."

"He probably didn't want to work," snapped my sister. "Bastard!"

My mother rapped her knuckles on the table.

"Sorry," said my sister.

"Your father wasn't the only one who couldn't find a job. There were plenty of people out of work. He decided to join the Navy, without telling me first. He signed up and the next thing I knew, he told me he was going away. I didn't know what I would do without him."

My mother's eyes filled with tears. We waited while she composed herself. As she started again, she began to twist a damp tissue in her hands.

"He promised to send for me. He said the Navy would find us a place to live, maybe even on the base. He said I could wait for him every time his ship came into port. He liked the idea. He wasn't allowed to take me with him during his basic training. When he finished his training, he came back for two weeks. When he left, I was pregnant. I saw him only once more after that, and that was all."

"How could he leave you," said my sister.

"I don't believe he intended to stay away. When he was here, this is where he wanted to be. When he was back on his ship, that's where he wanted to be. It was easy for him, at first, I think. He saw so many new things. The more he saw, the more he wanted to see."

"Whores," said my sister. Her voice rose. "I'll bet whores is what he was after."

"It became a matter of one thing or another. First, I was to wait until after the baby was born. Then, you were born, but there were bills to pay. He didn't even tell me I could go to any of the bases here in San Antonio to see the doctors. My daddy paid the hospital bills for the both of you. The bills your father had to pay turned out to be for a car he bought."

"Jesus!" exclaimed my sister.

"A year went by. Your first birthday came and went. Daddy took pictures that I sent to him. One day, he came back. He didn't write to say he was coming. I didn't know anything about it. One afternoon, there he was, on the porch. Knocking on the door. He said he had leave for a month because his ship would be going on a deployment of six months. I didn't know what to make of him coming back. I was angry and happy at the same time. He made it easy for me, though, by acting as if nothing had happened."

"I bet he did!" said my sister.

"He bought new linoleum for the living room and the kitchen. He fixed the window where one of the kids threw a baseball. The screen-door would never shut right. He scraped the bottom of it and it shut perfectly. What I remember most about the time he was here, is going out to eat. He didn't want me to cook. Luby's Cafeteria, he loved Luby's. The ship he was on, he said, was a feeder. The food at Luby's

was as good as he got on the ship. Every day, we'd eat at least once at
Luby's.

"He borrowed Daddy's car. Daddy didn't like it too much. He
needed it to get to work. Your father took Daddy to work in the morning, picked him up in the evening. The rest of the time, we had the
car.

"We'd drive around all over town, looking for restaurants. He insisted I bring you along. You were just starting to walk. He'd see a
place and he'd point and say, that one, I like the look of it. We have to
eat there. We'd go right then, or later that night, or maybe the next day.

"He also drove us around to look at houses. He said we should sell
the house—it wasn't even ours to sell—and buy one in a nicer neighborhood. It sounded to me like he wanted to stay home for good. He
actually wanted to call up the people who were selling the houses to ask
them if we could have a look, inside. I was too embarrassed. It was alright to listen to him talk, though. He was dreaming. I liked to dream
with him. Somehow, I knew nothing would come of it.

"He counted the days. There was a calendar on the wall, in the
kitchen, next to the stove. He'd sit at the table drinking coffee, staring at it. Every day. When he couldn't stand it anymore, he'd get up
and he'd put an X through the day, even though it wasn't over. I had
circled the last day of his leave.

"One day, there were still eight X's to go, he said he had to get back
to the ship. There were a lot of things that needed to be done before
the ship left. He couldn't let his shipmates do everything. He had to get
back and help. I don't believe that it was the reason. When he said it,
though, he believed it.

"We took a taxi to the bus station. We were early, about four hours
before the bus left. While we waited, he ate two hamburgers and a big
pile of french fries.

"When we came out of the restaurant, there were still three hours
before the bus left. We sat on one of the benches, there, at the bus
station. You were crying, making a nuisance of yourself. He couldn't sit
still. He circled the waiting area, went into the gift shop, went outside
where the passengers boarded the buses. When he finally returned, he
said I should go on home. No sense in all of us sitting there, waiting for
the bus.

"He wanted me to take a taxi back. I told him we had to watch our
money and that I'd better take a bus. He walked with me to the bus
stop. He didn't say goodbye. He didn't kiss me goodbye. He pulled on
the sleeve of your baby clothes and left when he saw the bus coming. I
haven't seen him since then.

"I found out I was pregnant again.

"A year went by, and a second, and then a third. It was always something. He always had an excuse. We couldn't afford it, was the one he used most. He was to have a homeport overseas. His enlistment was almost up and he would be home. He was supposed to get out on the day before his twenty-first birthday. I knew that much and waited for him to come home. He hadn't said anything about it. A week went by, then, it was two weeks. Still, he did not come home. I wrote to him, the letter was returned. Someone in the Navy post office had forwarded my letter to an address in Idaho. It was returned from there, unopened. So, he had been discharged. I learned that much."

"What was he doing in Idaho? Did he ever tell you?" I asked.

"Yes. Yes, he did, in fact. Years later. When he thought I wouldn't be hurt by it. He ran away with the wife of his best buddy. She happened to be from Idaho. He figured it would be the last place his buddy would go look for them. Which is where he found them. Your father's buddy forgave his wife and she went with him back to San Diego. When I heard from your father again, he had re-enlisted."

"What was his story, after he went in the Navy again, I mean?" said my sister.

"We both stopped pretending. I knew what he was up to. He had never told me an outright lie. Everything he ever told me was true. I mean, he actually believed it when he said it. If he continued with the pretense, he'd be lying. So, he stopped. I was glad. Daddy said if he ever came back, he was going to shoot him!"

"He should have!" said my sister.

"Daddy helped me to take care of you. When you kids got older, I went to work. All in all, things turned out well. I couldn't ask for better. I have no regrets."

"No thanks to him," said my sister.

"I wrote to him, over the years. To let him know how you two were doing. Sent pictures of you. I wrote to him, plenty of times, asking him to call. He could talk to you on the phone. He wouldn't do it."

"I wouldn't've talked to him," said my sister. "I have nothing to say to him. Which is more than I can say for some people."

"Come on, stop it," I said.

"He called. First time he ever did. He looked up the number in the telephone book because he asked me to identify myself. The voice sounded so familiar but I couldn't place it right away. He said he was retired, now. He had come home. The time went by so quickly."

"Bastard!" came the reply from my sister.

My mother rapped her knuckles on the table again.

"He said he wants me back and he won't stop until we're together again. All of us." My mother lit another cigarette.

"How can he even dare to think something like that after what he's done to us," my sister said. "You haven't given him any encouragement, have you?" This last directed to me.

"Of course, not," I said. "I've talked to him on the phone a few times and I've seen him twice. Make something of that."

"He's coming to your house. How nice and cozy," said my sister, sarcastically.

"I don't see the harm in it," I said, defensively.

"Leave him alone," my mother said to my sister. "Both of you have your feelings. I made a promise to myself, to never interfere with your feelings toward your father."

"But what about you?" asked my sister. "What are your feelings?"

"Whatever feelings I have for your father, I intend to keep them to myself. I will tell you this much. I am seeing someone."

"You are? You have a boyfriend? Great!" said my sister, enthusiastically.

"I wouldn't say he's a boyfriend," she said.

"I want to know everything."

"I think it's time to call the children in for dessert," said my mother.


Janice prepared a nice dinner for my father. A ham, with pineapple-raisin sauce. We had the neighbors take care of the kids for the first part of the evening. Janice didn't want them to intrude while we got acquainted. After dinner, I was to go get the kids. He could spend a little time with them before we put them to bed.

He never came. He didn't call to excuse himself, or to beg off; nothing. I became very upset. There is a form to these things, a form that ought to be observed. Janice, of course, was more tolerant. Maybe he got the address all wrong, she offered. When I had spoken to him, I neglected to get a number for him. He wasn't listed in the telephone book.

When it became evident that he wasn't coming, I went to get the kids while Janice served dinner for the two of us. My oldest, Phillip Junior, was just starting to talk. On the way home, he kept pulling on my hand, asking me for his grandfather.

I expected my father to call me at work, but he did not. Not a word from him for another two years. When he called, I again invited him to dinner at the house, telling him that he now had seven grandchildren, three of which he could see at my house. He said he didn't feel right about it. He laughed nervously and made a joke which I thought was uncouth. He said he wasn't much of a family man. Instead, he asked to meet me after work for drinks.

We met at what was obviously a singles bar and what was obviously a place frequented by people who were young enough to be his children. He had a woman with him, she was about thirty, thirty-five. She had the taut, parched color of someone who spends too much time in the sun. She smiled pleasantly and said she was pleased to meet me. The way she held on to her smile, a little too long, made me uncomfortable. From the movements of my father's upper arm, I could tell he was fondling her underneath the table.

Now that we both lived in the same town, my father didn't seem to be in such a hurry anymore. It probably had something to do with his retirement, as well. He was more relaxed and I found it easier to talk to him. He told me stories from his Navy days and I told him a few things about my work and a lot of things about my kids. Once or twice, he gave me the impression that he liked the kids, from what I told him, and maybe he wanted to see them. It was just an impression. He never asked to come to the house.


We began to make a habit of meeting for drinks each week, usually on a Wednesday. Wednesdays were good for me because Janice taught a course at the law school. The kids had a night out with the sitter.

He insisted that we meet each time at a different place. I'm a creature of habit. I preferred to meet in the hotel bars downtown, near my office. My father preferred bars full of young people, especially young women. Every week there was a new place that he wanted to check out.

It occurred to me, after we had been meeting for a little more than a year, that neither my father nor I particularly enjoyed each other's company. It was an obligation that we had contracted with one another. In the beginning of our bar meetings, we approached each other nervously, giving a perfunctory handshake. After a couple of months, we were comfortable enough with each other to dispense with the handshakes. We talked, but we never really said much to each other.

My mother and my sister never came up in our conversations. While he took pleasure in telling me about his Navy days, I half-suspected that he did it for the sake of reliving the pride of his youth. And while I had been a child, a teenager, a young man, an adult, during the same period, there was never a connection between us.


Since my father and my mother had spent so little time with each other and most of their lives apart, I naturally assumed that along the way their marriage had been dissolved. I had no exact memory of a divorce actually having occurred. I like things neat and tidy, so I was certain that they were divorced. It didn't seem reasonable to me that two people could live apart for so many years and still remain married to each other.

"I want to get married again," my mother announced one day.

"Mom! That's great! What wonderful news! May I ask who it is?"

"Oh, it's just someone that I met," trying hard to conceal the playfulness in her.

"Is it that same guy you were seeing and would never tell us about," said my sister.

"Is he nice, mother," Janice asked.

"That's great, Mom," I repeated.

"Hold on, all of you!" she said. "He's someone new. I've been seeing him for over a year now. He's very nice. At least, I think so. I didn't want any of you to meet him until I was sure. And, now I am." She beamed, biting her lower lip to keep from having her face consumed by a giant grin.

"When do we meet him?" Janice asked.

"Soon. I haven't decided how yet. I want it to be special. We both want it to be special. He wants your approval."

"Mom, it won't make any difference to us," said my sister.

"It does to him. It does to me, too," said my mother, gently.

Turning to me, she said, "Do you know Harvey Pelletier?"

"The lawyer? Not really. I've met him. Why?"

"He's going to represent me in the divorce," my mother said.

"What divorce? You mean ... " I was indeed surprised.

"You mean, you're still married to him?" my sister snarled in disgust.

"There was never any real reason to get a divorce. I thought he would come back some day. I wasn't sure of what I would do when he did. When he called and said he was back in town and he wanted to see me, I realized how much I had been living with his memory. It dawned on me that there was a part of my life that I had neglected. I decided to get serious about getting married again. Something made me want to live again."

"Pelletier's a good lawyer," I said. "Anyway, there won't be much to a divorce for you. It'll just be a matter of filing the papers."

"It's not quite that simple. The lawyer part of it is simple, I suppose. I wouldn't know about that," said my mother.

She lit a cigarette, tilting her head up to exhale toward the ceiling.

"Somebody has to tell your father," she said.

I knew immediately that she meant me, of course.

"He's got to hear it from one of you," she said.

"Why wouldn't you want to do it, mother," Janice asked, curious.

"Because I want no further contact with him. Phillip and Frances are his children. They will always be bound to him. I'm not. It's out of respect that I want it told to his face. And," she turned to me, "I want it done before Mr. Pelletier files the papers. I don't want him to first hear about it from a lawyer. I feel I owe him that much."

"You don't owe him a damned thing, Mom," said my sister. "If it were up to me, I'd just slap the son of a bitch with the papers. Let him know the world goes on." My mother and I frowned at her.

My mother blew the smoke out one side of her face, and turned to look at me. "Will you do it?"

And that is how I came to be in his apartment, with him swinging his arm in the air, drink in hand, shoulders thrown back, pacing in the narrow space between the loveseat and coffeetable.

"That don't mean nothing," he said. "Not in the long run, it don't mean nothing."

"She wants to get on with her life," I said.

"She can't do that," said my father. "I haven't had my chance to prove myself to her. I deserve my chance."

"You've been in town for a long time now and she won't even see you. You chase every skirt that crosses your path. I'd say it's pretty clear that you never wanted a chance to begin with," I said.

"Bullshit! All I need is a chance to see her, she won't be able to say no to me. Not if she sees me." He became excited.

"There's not much chance of that," I said.

"There is, if you help. How about it?"

"No, sir, I can't. If I could, and I don't think anybody can, I wouldn't."

"So, you're taking your mother's side in this?"

"There's not any sides to take. I'm afraid you don't have much of a choice, legally speaking," I told him. "I don't know if you want to hear this, but the time to prove yourself was long ago."

"You're saying I blew it."

"In a manner of speaking, yes," I said.

"Well, let's leave that part of it aside for the time being. What can I do to stop the divorce?"

"You're not listening to me. At this point, nothing. I say that as a lawyer."

"That's right, you're the wiseguy attorney, aren't you. What if you take me on as a client. I'll pay. Sure, that's the way to do it. We'll keep it strictly business. You can always use another client, hunh?"

"I don't practice that kind of law. Besides, lawyers shouldn't have relatives as clients," I said.

"What about that wife of yours? She's a lawyer, isn't she?"

"You don't really need a lawyer, sir. My mother will not be asking for anything from you. Nothing. Under the circumstances, it has not been a marriage for more than thirty years. The court will grant the divorce because it will decide to make legal what has been in fact the case. The two of you don't have a marriage."

"There's another man, isn't that right? That's the only possible reason she could want a divorce now."

"I believe there is, sir, but that's not the point. My mother wants to be legally unbound so she can pursue her own interests. At this point, it appears that you are in the way."

"Don't give me that shyster bullshit! I know what the point is. The point is another man. That is always the point."

"Well, in any case, you don't have any grounds to contest it. It'll be a waste of money for you to hire a lawyer, in my opinion. Just sign the papers when you get them. I'm surprised it took her this long to ask for one."

"You're telling me that all she has to do is ask for a divorce and she'll get one?"

"That's about it."


"I was planning on getting back with her, with your mother, you know? Sure, I was never much of a husband, or a father, for that matter. I know all of that. You should be able to understand how these things work. Smart college boy like you. You figure some guys are meant to be fathers, some are not. That's just the way things are. Doesn't take a college boy to figure that out.

"Time I found out about myself, you and your sister were already born. That was too fucking bad. Alright? It was too fucking bad. There was nothing I could do about it. Was there? It was too fucking late. You and your sister, born.

"So, you think I'm a cocksucker, desert you like that. Fine. Fine with me. I can't stop you, how you feel about me. Maybe you even got a right to. I don't know about that.

"I had my own life to think about. Okay, I fucked up. I really fucked up. I fucked things up for your mother. I fucked things up for you. I fucked things up for your sister. Fine. I fucking fucked up.

"There was nothing I could do to fix it. Sometimes, you fuck something up and you try to fix it and you end up fucking it up worse than what you fucked up to begin with. That's the way I called it.

"There was things that I had to do. I had already fucked up enough with your mother. There was no point in fucking things up for myself, too. I saw there was a chance for me. Only fucking chance I ever had. I'll tell you something, college boy, I didn't think twice. I took my fucking chance.

"I keep in touch, you know. In my own way. I send a little cash when I have it. Maybe I should've sent more, okay? Okay, I should've sent more. Maybe I should've helped with your college, you and your sister. I didn't. Live the way I do, takes money. All the fucking money I could get my fucking hands on.

"Anyway, things didn't turn out too bad, did they? Think back on it, things didn't turn out too bad. You didn't need me, did you? You did alright for yourself, fancy fucking lawyer. You got everything. Your sister, I hear, your sister's got a good husband. Nice kids. She's got everything.

"What the fuck is the beef here? What's to complain about? I got my living out of the way. You know what it takes to actually live out your life, man. Fucking wiseguy like you, you know what it takes? Do you know what it takes?

"I got a few years left, I figure. There's no reason not to pick things up with your mother. I always meant to do that. She probably won't believe me, but it's true. She married me once, that has to mean something. There are certain things you can't just throw away, you know? I never had any trouble getting the women I want. I don't see where your mother has to be any different. I got her once, I can get her again."

"My mother isn't just any woman. She's not like the others you're used to, I hope you understand that," I said.

"Who the fuck made you the expert, wiseguy? Sure, your mother's like the rest of them. Take it from me," he said.

"In that case," I said, "I don't think you ought to talk about her like that. At least, not to me."

"Yeah, you're right," he said, calming down. "Sorry, kid. All I need is a chance."

"I think it's too late."

"Doesn't matter. It's not too late. Even if she gets married again, I won't stop. Gettin' married don't mean nothing. Not in the long run. Not in the long run, it don't mean nothing."

# A Sandwich at Blimpy's

The Blimpy's in Greenwich Village teemed with its daily lunchtime crowd. The noisy chatter in the room came largely from the workers behind the counter who made a big production of rushing to and fro. They shouted orders across the make-up line. They yelled to a processing area in back to replenish supplies. Each shout was more urgent than the one before, designed of course to flatter and impress the customer.

"Quick! Quick! This beautiful lady has been waiting a long time!"

"Hurry! This gentleman has to go back to work!"

"Come on! Come on! Come on! Can't you see this boy is starving? Look at his face!"

All of it, the exaggerated bustle, the yelling, had little effect on the slow line of customers. They kept their faces immobile, moving at a measured pace. They held their trays tightly, oblivious to the histrionics of the serving line.

Most of them were regulars who would eat at the same restaurant on the same day each week. Some of them reserved one day, usually a Friday, a payday Friday, for a new place, or a more expensive one. These regulars were accustomed to Blimpy's, the shenanigans of the workers.

The stock company behind the counter could fill three orders at once, after which they took orders from three more customers, and the let's-put-on-a-show noisy rush would begin again.

The tourists were awestruck by the spectacle. They kept their eyes on the performance behind the counter. It was to these customers, the once-in-a-lifetime visitors to New York, that the workers played. It would be something to bring back home, to relive among incredulous faces in the warmth of a winter evening or a long summer's afternoon.

The natives of New York made use of their indifference by turning to look over the eating area and scanning with the radar of experience for a place at a table. The adventure of the noon hour was finding a place to sit and eat.

Blimpy's regular customers came from the shops and brownstone offices nearby. There were actors, dancers, singers, and musicians who waited for the big break. Writers, playwrights, and philosophers who thrived on the cheap lunch. There were students, too, from NYU, a few blocks away.

But, by far, the most interesting were the tourists. The tourists were easily identifiable. Their eyes tended to remain wide open, constantly alert for the sudden occurrences of notorious New York. They knew to be careful, not to stare at anyone for too long. Back home, to stare was impolite. In New York, their intuition told them, eye contact, to stare, would be threatening. It could be taken as a challenge, an invitation to violence. They had been warned about pursesnatchers, pickpockets, and panhandlers; prostitutes and junkies; all manner of human beings unlike those to be found in the cities and towns where they came from. New York was a place in which to be wary.

The couple in front of Lennie Uriegas was from Kansas, or Indiana, or from some place flat and of minor population. A place where their friends, neighbors, and business associates looked up to them. As they stood in the line, Lennie could see that they had the airs of important people.

The massive population of New York and the fact that they were visiting for just a short time, made them feel relatively insignificant, an experience they would not have anticipated. They found themselves in an anonymity to which they were not accustomed and which they were reluctant to accept.

Welcome to the universe, thought Lennie.

He noted the way the important midwestern couple searched the faces of the serving line people for a signal of the deference owed to them, a recognition of their station in life. They had not felt like this on their trips to Chicago.

Lennie concluded the worst part of it for them must be the experience of virtual isolation in the midst of millions of people. To walk among faces that did not see them, to brush against bodies that recoiled at the least contact.

The aloneness must be unbearable for them, Lennie thought. Yet the man and the woman seemed anxious to distinguish themselves, to set themselves apart. They had eyes that announced, we are not part of this crowd, we are not like them at all. We belong elsewhere!

Not bad, thought Lennie. He repeated the phrases several times over so as not to lose them. The repetition would help him to hold on to the phrases until he got his sandwich and found a place to sit. He'd jot them down in his notebook, under the rubric, "Ideas for Songs."

"Blimpy ate hamburgers, I tell you!" The man complained to his wife. He had an air about him, with voice to match, of a man of unbounded knowledge and moral superiority. He knew the quiddity of what.

"You mean, the one from the Popeye cartoons?" the man's wife said.

"Exactly!" the man confirmed in a voice loud and ringing, which swerved into the din behind the counter and disappeared finally into the indifference of those waiting in line. Only Lennie, the collector of the odd phrases and the mannerisms of itinerant humans, paid attention.

"There are no hamburgers on the menu," the man continued. "You can see for yourself. Up there! Do you see any hamburgers on that menu?"

"Perhaps they have another Blimpy in mind, dear," the man's wife said.

"Of course, they don't. There's only one Blimpy and he eats hamburgers. I expected a menu with hamburgers on it," said the man, becoming impatient and petulant.

"Then, let's go some place where you can order a hamburger, dear," said the man's wife, patiently, unperturbed.

"That is quite beside the point," said the man. "Anyone who knows and understands advertising formulas, knows better than to trifle with them."

The man turned, expecting to accept impressed looks from listeners close by. As the man's gaze swept across Lennie's face, Lennie let his face fall into an inscrutable mask.

"Yes, dear," the man's wife said.

The man began to mimic the cartoon character. " 'If you let me have a hamburger today, I will gladly pay you on Friday!' That's Blimpy for you!" the man beamed, smiling in his self-importance. Again, he turned to receive the appreciative looks to which he was accustomed. A man of small town wit would be another note for Lennie's notebook.

"I think it was Tuesday," said his wife, tired and meek, almost under her breath. There was a lifetime of reacting to her husband's excesses in the way she measured her voice. There was, Lennie noted, a slight calculation in her remark, evidence that she knew how far to go in contradicting her husband.

"What was Tuesday?" her husband asked, thrown off-guard by his wife's comment. As she was not about to repeat herself, he quickly lost interest in what she had to say, confident that it was he who had made the pertinent remark. He was a man who demanded, or at least, expected, prompt acquiescence and automatic approval for everything he had to say.

The man made a half-turn to face the serving line, crossing his arms over his barrel chest and basket belly. He had made his point and he was content.

Lennie and the man's wife exchanged glances. She snapped her face away quickly.

"Tuesday," the man's wife said, spurred by a perverse refusal to let her husband's inaccuracy stand. Later, in the safety of their hometown, she would say to herself, and then repeat to her closest friends, that had they not been in New York, she would not have corrected him. She would say, I don't know what came over me.

"Blimpy would gladly pay on Tuesday. Not Friday. I think you should know that, dear." Her voice trailed off, a thin little smile the only sign of her satisfaction.


Lennie waited in the line, behind the midwestern couple, patiently slapping his notebook against his thigh. He repeated phrases and formed observations into words so he could remember to record them for later use. He tried to imagine the guitar chords that could accompany the phrase, "contentious amor." Unconsciously, he slipped into the chords for "Careless Love."

The midwest woman turned to look at Lennie, as if the slight triumph over her husband had emboldened her. Having vanquished her husband, she was ready for other challenges. The stare she had for Lennie slithered along the ridge of her nose, slow and oppressive, before it precipitously dropped at his feet. Lennie felt the bluntness of the stare, knew its wellspring and its meaning. He had received it often enough from his teachers, from passersby in the street.

He knew full well what the stare meant and he had learned what to do with it, how to return it, how to give as good as he got, in fact, to give better than he got.

While the stare of the woman was cold and unblinking, with an undefinable fear lurking beneath, Lennie's stare smoldered, displaying in the slight twitch of facial muscles, an implacable capacity for violence.

The woman became uncomfortable when she received Lennie's stare. It was more than she had bargained for. The chill that passed through her body shoved her closer to her husband. Once she had turned away from him, Lennie saw the back of her neck erupt in a red flush.

She must think I'm a Puerto Rican rapist, thought Lennie.

When it was his turn to order, Lennie asked for a basic Blimpy sandwich and a side order of sliced tomatoes. The sandwich consisted of paper thin sheets of salami, ham, cheese, and lettuce shredded into a colorless filigree over the meat. To this, the workers added a liberal spray of olive oil and vinegar. The tomato slices cost a nickel more.

For the third Blimpy of the week, thought Lennie, tomatoes are not necessarily an extravagance. Besides, he cheered himself, there should be some money in the mail soon.

Lennie's sandwich was next up on the runway. He edged along the line, standing with his tray held level, slightly above his belly button. His notebook was clasped under his arm. Lennie swerved his head slowly, gazing over the heads of the diners, to catch a glimpse of someone about to leave. He had begun observing people's mannerisms as a game to keep himself occupied. In time, he had gotten to where he could recognize certain gestures, movements, inadvertent signals, and he was able to calculate within a few seconds when a person would get up from one of the tables.

The obvious ones were those who were on a last bite of their sandwiches, heads bent low, eyes flitting from side to side, in the posture of a sprinter ready for the gun. There were others who finished in such a way that told him they would linger at the table to smoke a cigarette, or if in a group, to chat.

There were those who could not force themselves to eat an entire sandwich. The trick for Lennie was to figure how much of the sandwich they would eat. Occasionally, he was thrown for a loop by someone who called a busboy to bring a doggie bag. His taxonomy of eaters included dress, likely occupation, body shape and movement.

As he scanned the room, he spied two who appeared ready to leave. If he could get through the line in time, he could claim the table before it was cleared. The busboys could clean around him. The midwestern man and woman would not be fit competition in the short dash to be seated. They would insist on a clean table. The couple in front of the midwestern duo would wait for a table by themselves. Lennie could read the office affair in their faces. He wondered whether they had been to bed more than twice in the last month. Another idea for a song.

As might be expected, and it was something he ought to have counted on, the tourist couple insisted upon giving the Pakistani cashier exact change. The man painstakingly ironed flat the dollar bills before laying them on the man's outstretched hand and then dropped each coin into the man's hand, in such a way as to keep from touching him. He kept a running sub-total, virtually shouting it out each time, as if each decibel level might improve the probability that the foreigner would comprehend and follow his addition.

Lennie paid for his sandwich and soda and came up beside the midwestern couple. He was stalking now. The man at the table he had his eye on was almost ready. The couple moved back and to one side, gaining some distance from him, retreating to stand behind him near the cash register. They were going to wait for a table to be cleaned; and, by God, they intended to sit by themselves.

They probably will wait a long time, thought Lennie. Good fucking luck. Lennie had long ago stripped his expectations down to only a chair and small flat surface for his food and his open notebook.

Lennie had pegged his mark correctly. New York called upon its citizens, even temporary ones like Lennie, to be constantly alert and resourceful. Swiftly, with the moves of a practiced ballroom dancer, Lennie glided through the narrow passages, past several tables, until he gracefully dipped his body to lower his tray upon the table just as the man and his companion stood up. Neither of them reacted to Lennie's advance. They didn't even see him.

As he sat down, a young girl scooted up and lowered her tray into the space across from him. She sat down and looked at Lennie.

"You're pretty slick," she said, smiling, adjusting to a comfortable position in the chair. "I was watching you. Pretty good moves. You could be a waiter, if you had the ambition."

"You're not too bad yourself," he said, not bothering to lift his face to look at her. He was busy with his pre-prandial rituals. "It's not easy to get a table in this place," he added absently.

Lennie busied himself with picking up the residue of the previous diners, dumping it on the tray he brought. He moved it as far to his right as he could without tipping it over. He kept his notebook in his lap until the busboy, appearing mysteriously, swept by, taking the tray and refuse with him. Under the table, he opened the notebook to an appropriate page, and then placed it on the table where the tray had been. He arched his back to dig in his pocket for a pen. After all that was done, Lennie finally turned his face to look at the girl.

Lennie forced a smile for her and leaned back in his chair to unwrap his sandwich. The sandwich paper and the edges of the bottom slice of the bun were soggy with the oil, vinegar, and the excrescence of water from the shredded lettuce.

The girl unwrapped her sandwich as if she were following Lennie's lead. She made a face, wrinkling her nose, holding her hands in front of her, fingers spread apart. Just touching the paper wrapper had made her hands oily and smelly with vinegar. Lennie placed one of his napkins on her tray.

"People never get enough napkins," Lennie observed.

She twirled the napkin around each of her fingers.

"Why do they put Italian dressing on these things? It's a funny way to make a sandwich," she said.

"Dry," said Lennie, watching her closely.

The girl finished wiping her hands and wadded up the napkin. She

tossed it in front of her sandwich. With the tip of her lacquered fingernail, she tipped over the bun to inspect the contents.

"The salami and the cheese are too dry. Salty, too. You might choke
on it," said Lennie without smiling. "In fact, you will probably choke on
it."

"You're kidding. I mean, you're making a joke, right?" she said,
tilting her head to one side so the smooth line of her raven hair broke
into a soft curl on her shoulder. There was a small grouping of lines in
the middle of her forehead as she raised her eyebrows.

"Suit yourself," said Lennie, shrugging his shoulders. "Don't say you
weren't warned, though."

The girl became curious, smiling broadly. Her lips were plump and
full, just short of a pout. They were covered in a bright scarlet, through
which peered even, white, teeth. She leaned over the table as if she and
Lennie were involved in some conspiracy.

"Do people really choke on these things? I mean, if people actually choke on these things, why do you come here?" She looked at her
sandwich, apprehensive of it, as if trying to find the courage to take a
bite.

The girl scraped the strings of lettuce away from their resting place
over the sliced meat, pushing them together into a neat little pile on the
tray beside the bottom half of the sandwich. She lifted a slice of salami,
rolled it into a loose cigar-shape before taking a small bite. Then she
tore a bit of the cheese slice to nibble on. She continued to gaze at
Lennie as she picked single strings of lettuce which she sucked into her
mouth.

Her lipstick is much too red, thought Lennie.

"Don't let Blimpy see you do that," said Lennie, a smile crossing his
lips.

"See what? Who's Blimpy? Why would he care?" she said.

"Blimpy is a legend, a man honored and revered for his ability to eat.
A phagodirigible. If anybody is what he eats, it's Blimpy," said Lennie.

"Is he here? Where is he?" she said, craning her neck to look over
the diners, curious, intrigued.

"Blimpy is actually a cartoon character. Didn't you ever see Popeye
when you were little?" said Lennie, drily. "Were you ever little?"

"You gave me the distinct impression that Blimpy is a person who
owns this place," she said. "You're making fun of me, aren't you? You're
trying to confuse me. You can make fun of me, but don't confuse me. I
don't like it when I'm confused."

"You think I said Blimpy comes here. I said nothing of the kind.
People hear only what they want to hear. That way they're saved from
the unhealthy practice of listening to what other people have to say,"

Lennie said. He picked up half of his sandwich in two hands, took a big bite. His stuffed cheeks bulged as he chewed.

"I just thought there might be someone called, Blimpy. I mean, my brother had a best friend that everybody called Tarzan. If somebody was nicknamed Blimpy for all of his life, he probably ate a lot, and so, it would be natural for him to open up a restaurant and call it Blimpy's, don't you think? That makes sense to me. So, I just assumed ... "

She picked up the loosely tubed slice of salami, wadded it up, toyed with it before putting all of it in her mouth.

"Never mind, I'm sorry," said Lennie as he swallowed. After he wiped his mouth, he said, "Does that happen to you often?"

"What?"

"Getting confused. Is it easy for you to get confused?"

"No. I mean, yes. I mean, today. Just today. There's a lot of things on my mind today. Other days, maybe not."

"So, you're not paying much attention to anything today," Lennie said.

"Not really. I just came in here to have something to eat. I didn't expect to find the son of the Great Deceiver making fun of me." She didn't sound offended or cross with Lennie.

"It's great sport in the Village, actually. Abandon all hope ye who enter here. Play jokes on the tourists. Torment them in the name of fun." Lennie took another bite of his sandwich.

"It shows? I mean, it shows that I'm a tourist?" the girl asked.

"Not only a tourist, but I would say, a Texas tourist?" Lennie said, enunciating the question at the last moment.

"Very good. Are you one of those who have a knack for people's accents? Do you know a place called San Antonio?" She asked.

"Sure. The place where John Wayne died for our sins. So did Richard Widmark and Laurence Harvey. On the plus side, Joan Crawford was born there."

"What about you?" She ate another piece of salami and cheese.

"Corpus Christi, the Riviera of Texas, the Emerald City, Sparkling City by the Sea."

She smiled in genuine surprise. "We're practically neighbors. Another Texan, I don't believe this. I thought you were Puerto Rican or Cuban."

Lennie leaned across the table, placing an erect forefinger over his pursed lips. "Not so loud. The lady over there, see the one in the coral blouse?"

"Which one? Is it the one who looks like she's lonesome for Toto?"

"One and the same. It's not likely she's ever seen a Mexicano. So, she's convinced I'm a Puerto Rican and therefore a menace to society.

I think she saw *West Side Story* and that's about all she needs to know."

"That's awful. We need to stand up for our heritage. I think I'll go over there right now and straighten her out, what do you think?" she said, smiling playfully.

"No, don't. Let her go on with what she thinks. It would be a sorry world if people knew only the truth and nothing else. Being wrong, ignorant, has its benefits and pleasures." Lennie looked straight into her eyes, arched his brows at her a couple of times, then he smiled.

"You think lying is better? You prefer that people live a deception, rather than know the truth?" she asked.

"No, I don't mean that at all. You see, a lie is only a lie until you discover the truth. When you don't know any better, a lie is the same as the truth," said Lennie.

"That might work for a little while, but eventually, the truth has to come out," said the girl.

"Not necessarily. We'd be a lot better off, sometimes, not knowing the truth."

"Give me an example," she said, listening intently.

"How about the man who cheats on his wife?"

"Okay. We're all adults here."

"The wife asks, 'Are you cheating on me?' The husband says, 'No way!' She says, 'There's lipstick on your shorts and there is a pair of panties under the front seat of the car.' He says, 'Who're you going to believe?' She thinks. Nice home, two car garage, three kids, color TV, and he's got a nice pension coming when he retires. She says, 'I'm sorry. I should've never doubted you.'"

"But, he was cheating, right?"

"Who knows. Anyway, it doesn't matter. He said he wasn't and that's what's important. She probably doesn't believe him at all. The two of them will behave as if it didn't happen. Between the two of them, they have agreed upon a certain truth."

"What about the woman he was cheating on her with? She knows the truth, doesn't she?"

"Who knows. Suppose she's married as well and wants to stay that way. So, now, you have three people who swear nothing happened. They have accepted truths for reasons that are important to them. Only to themselves. The circumstances of their lives determine what is truth. It's not up to us to interfere with them."

"That's just a common sense situation. You make it sound as if people have nothing better to do than sit around and decide, this is true and this is a lie. I don't believe people say to themselves, I know this is a lie but I will live with it as though it is the truth. People just live their lives, they aren't bothered by whether something is true or false. They go along with things. This feels good, that feels not so good. That's what it's all about."

"It's too much of a feelgood world. That's what makes it suck," said Lennie, disgusted.

"Things can't be that desperate," said the girl, inclining her face.

"No, not desperate. I wouldn't say that. But, it sucks just the same."

In the pause that followed, Lennie set to work on the second half of his sandwich. The girl continued to pick up and nibble on pieces of the meat, cheese, and lettuce. Lennie continued to look at her with a fixed grin on his face. She avoided his look, getting trapped by it several times, which caused her to dart a glance to the side or down into her tray. She wiped her mouth and forcefully threw the napkin on the tray. She pushed her chair back a little.

"You're not leaving," said Lennie.

"I really should be going," said the girl.

"We just met. Stay, why don't you?"

Her face softened a little and she stuck out her arm across the trays for Lennie to shake. Her smile was wide and friendly and Lennie was swept up into its genuine warmth.

"My name's Belinda," she said, when Lennie took her hand in his. "Gutierrez," she added.

"Belinda Gutierrez," repeated Lennie, savoring the sound of it.

He made a move to withdraw his hand, but she held on to it, tugging at him.

"Not until you tell me your name," she said.

"Leonardo. People call me Lennie. From the Uriegas of Corpus Christi," he said.

"The Uriegas of Corpus Christi? Are there a lot of them?"

"Not many and too many. You figure my grandfather had one son, my father, and six daughters, my aunts. That makes a handful of us who are Uriegas. If you put all my aunts and cousins in alphabetical order, they take up about half the phone book."

Lennie took another bite of his sandwich. He saved the bite-sized heel to mop up the vinegar and oil that had not soaked into the paper.

"So, you live here, or something?" said Belinda. "I mean, the way you make fun of me, you're not a tourist, too, are you?"

"Two years. I'm a new breed of human being. Call us, Neo-New Yorkers," said Lennie.

"Neo-New Yorkers? Is that supposed to be clever?" she asked.

"Yeah, why not?"

"Just asking."

"I live four blocks that way, across Houston. Except, here, they pronounce it, 'Howston.' I always pronounce it the way we do at home. New Yorkers can be pretty perpendicular," said Lennie.

"What do you do here? Are you a writer? You're a writer, I bet."

"What makes you say that?"

"You talk like someone who loves words. Your own words." She smiled. Lennie couldn't be sure if she was teasing him.

"In a way, you're right. I use words for my songs. I'm a writer of songs. What's more, a wizard of the guitar. And, Still more, sad to say, a failed pianist."

"You're too young to be a failure," said she, sincerely.

"Virtuosos make it by age twelve or not at all. Failure comes early."

"Twelve years old? That's kind of young to be a failure, isn't it?"

"I was good enough to play in a rock and roll band, though."

"But, you chose to become a failed pianist anyway, right? Why?"

"You come away with more honor if you fail for lack of genius. If it turns out you're not a genius, it's not your fault."

"Is that more important? The honor of a failed genius?"

"Who wants to be a successful mediocrity."

"You could make a lot of money and then it wouldn't matter what people think."

"All you get when you have a lot of money is a lot of people kissing your ass. You ever wonder why custom places a man's wallet in a pocket over his ass?"

"You're getting crude," Belinda toyed with the straw from her soft drink.

"I'm also a crackerjack salesman of Mexican jewelry. Silver earrings, necklaces, and trinkets. You name it."

"There is shop over there somewhere, in one of those narrow little streets, Oaxaca, or something. I saw it. Is that where you crackerjack your salesman stuff."

"Right you are! I wear a vest made from a zarape when I work. It's the key to my success as a crackerjack salesman. In sales, appearance is everything. The vest says it all."

"The vest, a family heirloom?" When Lennie didn't answer right away, Belinda said, "Sure it is! Of course, you come from a long line of crackerjack salesmen?"

"No, Rico, the guy I work for, he owns it. Comes with the job. I inherited it from hundreds of others who have worked for Rico. Fact is, nobody stays working for Rico for very long."

"He must be some taskmaster," Belinda said, frowning, shaking her head from side to side. "Is he from Oaxaca?"

"Rico? No, not from Oaxaca. He's a Rico from the Bonacelli's of Brooklyn. Everyone of his aunts and uncles has a Rico in the family. Now, before you ask, let me tell you about friend Rico. Seems that, as a small boy, Rico dreamed of being in that home-grown organization that nobody calls the Mafia. Leg-breaking, an entry-level position, is an old and honorable profession in Brooklyn, one practiced by various of Rico's relatives. Cousins, and the like. However, fate took Rico's family in a different direction altogether. Rico's dad and his brothers are garage mechanics. Not one to be deterred by such humble beginnings, Rico decided to follow in his cousin's footsteps. Restore the family honor, as it were. He tried to hire on with the Mafia. Out of respect for his family wishes, they wouldn't take him on."

"You make them sound like decent people," Belinda said, lowering her head.

"They might be, for all I know. Anyway, that's what Rico told me," said Lennie, defiantly. "Rico decides to become a free-lance leg-breaker. Sort of establish an independent reputation and then his relatives have to hire him."

"Prove himself first."

"Right. The only jobs he can get are for some small-timers. Scavengers who don't threaten anyone. Turns out, the guys Rico works for are real scumbags. They do business with the Blacks, out in Brownsville. Rico's relatives never heard of equal opportunity regardless of race, color, or creed."

"Can't the federal government do something about that?"

"So, Rico's cousin, Rico Bonacelli, tells him he can't do that. There's important people very upset with him. I forgot to tell you that he did this after school. Part time. He graduated from high school as a favor to his mother, and probably to keep his father from killing him. Rico's not too clear on that. When he graduated, he was about to become a free-lance tough guy on a full time basis. That's about when he got the message."

"You mean, they just tell him, don't do that, and he obeys?"

"Sure. Rico's not too smart, but he's smart enough to know he could get his own legs broken."

"What a sad, tragic story."

"All stories about dreams thwarted are sad, but not tragic. Rico found himself out of a career even before he got started. He was a year out of high school, didn't have a job, no prospects. One day, Rico becomes the disgrace of his neighborhood by letting his mother nag him into going to college."

"He could have joined the French Foreign Legion. Couldn't a college graduate from Brooklyn fit right in with cutthroats and murderers?"

"Without trying too hard, he makes it through college. He took teacher courses. When he graduates, he becomes a high school teacher. Not a very good one, sad to say. It was obvious from he beginning that he was not going to make it. So, friend Rico is facing a double disgrace. He wasn't allowed to become a mafioso and he's too much of a shithead to be a teacher. Fortunately, he taught far away from his neighborhood and was able to travel that road of shame all by himself."

"Away from the scorn of the neighborhood and the grieving eyes of his poor mother," said Belinda.

"That's right. So, my employer and now friend, Rico, began to take acid and several other illegal substances that produce alternate modes of consciousness. Of course, none them did him very much good, but they did give him insight into certain commercial possibilities. He discovers what his relatives in Brooklyn already know. Illegal commerce is profitable commerce. It's all right there to be had if someone is careful and if someone doesn't mind taking a little risk."

"A college-educated mind in action is a wondrous thing."

"Indeed, it is. He was fired from his teaching job at about the same time that he decided to become a dope smuggler."

"I saw something like that in a movie once. One big score and get out of it, right?"

"That was probably Rico's plan. Rico's not real bright, as I said, but he's not dumb, either. Anyway, we cut to Oaxaca where we pick up Rico waiting for delivery of his merchandise. He thought he would go down to Mexico, get the stuff, come right back, and be rich. All inside of twenty-four hours."

"He's in and out of the business before anyone knows."

"His plan, exactly. They make him wait six days, though. He gets nervous, makes a call to find out what the fuck's going on. He's told to get the hell out of there. Somebody knew something Rico did not know. He's on his way out of the country when the cops pick him up. He had the money with him. They take the money and they tell Rico to get the hell out of town."

"Wait, don't tell me," said Belinda, eagerly, moving forward over the table. "See if I can get it. Your friend and employer Rico gets into trouble with the people who loaned him the money that the Mexican police took. They probably think he's telling them the truth, but that doesn't matter. They want their money. Your friend Rico is now up shit creek! Right?"

"You got it. He can't even make the vigorish on it. He goes to his cousins for help. He doesn't expect them to give him the money, but he figures they might put in a good word with the very pissed-off people who want their money."

"His cousins tell him he should have kept his nose clean," Belinda said.

"Not quite," said Lennie. "They tell him it's territory. If they get involved, it becomes a jurisdictional dispute. Lamentably, they tell him, nothing can be done to help him. He should have checked with them before he getting into it."

"There's nothing like having professional advice before you need it," said Belinda.

"You said it. Lucky for Rico, his mother died and left him the family house. Don't ask why she did that. The house had been in her family for three, four generations. She left it to him. Rico, now of the landed gentry, sees the house as a quick way to raise the cash he needs to get rid of his very nasty problem."

"He's going to sell the house and throw his father out into the street?"

"Better than that. He wants to sell the house to his father. You can imagine how his father reacts when Rico offers to sell him the house. His father says, 'Whaddaya mean, buy da house? I focking live heah, don't I. What the fock!'"

"Then what?"

"Rico knows his father's going to go for the house. He needs some subtle encouragement. So, he goes to a real estate agent. The real estate agent puts a for sale sign on the stoop. The father comes home, sees it, and grabs Rico. 'What the fock,' he says. Rico says, 'I need the fucking money, pop.' His father says, "Why ain't you said nothing? You need focking money, you come to me. How much you need, tell me.' 'Twenty-five thousand,' says Rico. 'I focking killya foist,' says his father."

"I like Rico's father," said Belinda.

"Rico tells him he's in trouble and needs the cash real bad. A business deal that went bad. His father, 'You been hangin' out wit you cousin Rico, ain't dat right? I'll focking kill'im. You uncle promise nonna ma focking boys ain't gettin' in da focking business. You foist, den I kill you focking cousin.' Rico knows then that he has his father's attention. It was just a matter of time. His father had to get used to the idea, that's all."

"Families are great, aren't they?"

"Rico's father finally says, 'I ain't gonna buy my own focking house. I don't care it belonged to ya focking granmudda, may the focking worms take an eternal focking piss over huh miserable focking bones.' 'You just gonna give me the money, pop?' Rico's hopeful. 'Fock no! That money is what ya mudda, rest in peace, and me was gonna live on in Florida when I give up the shop to Teddy.' Rico says, 'you ain't going down there to Florida by yourself, are you, pop?' 'I'm gonna die in dis house, jes like she did,' says his father.

"Rico said he would've felt sorry for his father except that he was so close to getting the money, and that occupied all of his mind at the moment. 'You gonna sell da house to you brother, Alphonse,' Rico's father says. 'I'll sell you the house, pop, but not Alphonse. Where the fuck is Alphonse going to get the money,' says Rico. 'I already been to da bank. You cousin, Luca, dat works in da bank, Luca says, leave everything to me, Uncle Rico. He's a good boy, Luca, you shoulda been like him. He says you get maybe forty grand, what the house is worth. I stand up for Alphonse, Alphonse pays the bank. You get yo focking money.'

"Fat fucking chance,' says Rico. His father says, 'Alphonse is a good focking boy. Don't say nuttin' bout Alphonse. He got'im four kids awready. They move inna house, you move you focking ass out! 'Alphonse is a fucking pussy, pop!' says Rico. 'He'll never pay the bank and you know it.' 'Well, somebody's gotta look after him,' his father says.

"Sounds like a sweet old man," Belinda said.

"Yeah, I guess," said Lennie. "Rico then pays up on the money he owes and he's got a whole bunch left over. He had enough to go back to Oaxaca, he's got traveler's checks this time, buys all the silver junk he can get his hands on. With the inventory as collateral, he gets a loan to open up the shop. What more proof could you ask for. The American system really and truly works!"

"Sounds like Rico's a man twice blessed. Plus, he's got you working for him, on top of all that! How did you get into this inspiring enterprise of Rico's?"

"I was walking down the street, broke and miserable. Rico yells out, 'Hey, you, come here. You can pass for a Mexican, you want a job?'"

"And all along, you thought you were somebody else, right? Thought you left being a Mexican behind you in Texas." Belinda grinned.

"No, not really. I don't really have any problems with being Mexican. What the hell else am I going to be? I never expected that just because I happen to be Mexican, it's enough to land me a job. That was a new one on me. I really did need the job. Right then and there, I took the job. Rico makes me put on the vest. Instantly, I become the Mexican salesman."

"A job you were born for."

"Talent is mysterious in its manifestations. My contribution to Rico's business is the sidewalk speakers that play Mexican music. I choose the music. The tourists love it."

"I believe you're a good salesman. I mean, just listening to you, I can tell. However, you're really not a salesman at all, are you? Salesman is what you do and not what you are. After work, when you strip away the zarape vest, you become who you really are. A songwriter. Is that what you said? So, tell me, who sings your songs?"

"I do, mostly, who else? I actually sold a song last year. To a very important and promising singer. He used to knock'em dead over at the Bitter End. He got a recording contract and he discovered my music. All at once."

"How fortuitous."

"Damned right!"

"What happened then?"

"Nothing happened then. It looked like something was about to happen. What happened is the son of a bitch fell in love with an actress, a harridan twice his age who was called out to Hollywood to play somebody's mother in a television show."

"Which one?"

"Shit, I don't know? I don't have a television. He was supposed to show up for a recording session here in New York and he never did. It wasn't till a couple of weeks later that anyone knew anything about what happened to him. Even then all we found out is she took him with her. They said she couldn't live without him."

"You don't believe it, though. You're going to tell me you don't believe in love."

"Of course, I believe in love. It should be kept within the same species, though."

"As you get older you become a different species? Or, are actresses and singers of a different species?"

"Actors! They tell me he quit being a singer so he could devote himself to her career. I guess we can figure out which part of her career he was taking care of."

"You sound bitter."

"No. Yeah. Maybe you're right. Let's say he sincerely fell in love with her. The irony of it all is my song of love was killed by love."

"Couldn't you sell the song again? Get somebody else to record it?"

"I don't know. Nobody's been interested. Nobody's knocking down my door to get at my songs, you know."

"That's too bad. Despite all that, all the ups and downs ... "

"Mostly, downs."

" ... you keep writing songs. You're a wizard of the guitar."

"Yeah, I play my guitar like a wizard. I even organized a mariachi band. I was going to introduce Mexico, authentic Mexico, to New York

City. Easy music, easy money. I figured, if the tourists buy Mexican trinkets, they might listen to Mexican music, too."

"A blend of commerce and art," Belind a said.

"I ask around the neighborhood and pretty soon I got four musicians. I had about fifty dollars, saved it up, and I spent it mostly on sandwiches and beer for the band. One of the guys was a black trumpet player, a hotshot who went to Juilliard."

"I'm impressed."

"I got them all together and I played some records for them. We agreed it wouldn't take much to get pretty good at it. I should have known there was going to be trouble when the guy from Juilliard says he can't get into it unless he has some sheet music. Sheet music!"

"You couldn't go to the music store and buy some?"

"Shit, no! I wrote a couple things down for him and the two of us practiced separately. I got him to where he could do something passable. It was a little stiff, you understand, but I didn't figure anyone would notice. We finished rehearsing after a month and we were ready. I even wrote some new songs, you know, in Spanish. I was going to do the singing. The group was ready."

"And?"

"We got one job. We lasted for one job."

"New York was not ready for mariachi music, I take it?"

"I don't know, maybe not. We didn't play long enough to ever find out. There's a Cuban restaurant, a couple of blocks over, La Mata de la Habana. We call it, Cuban Roots. The guy that owns it decided to give us a chance. What the hell, no one knows or cares, from Mexican music, he said."

"He doesn't sound like a very good Cuban, hunh?"

"The guy's from New Orleans. Never set foot in Cuba in his life. I think his father or grandfather came from there, long time ago. Well, he gave us a chance, you know. Gotta give him that."

"Of course."

"Get this. It's our first night. Good crowd for an audience. Lot of people bunched up at the bar waiting for a table. There's a buzz in the room. We start to play. The black trumpeter son of a bitch figures he's got a chance to do an audition in case there's somebody important in the audience, which is not hardly since it's mostly tourists in there on a weekend."

"How can he do that, you rehearsed, right?"

"The band is trying to play 'Jalisco,' and the trumpet player goes along with it for a little while, and then he ends up doing jazz. He sounded good, too. The more I tried to get him back to playing what we were supposed to be playing, the more it sounded like we were interfering with him. Couple of people in the audience told us to ease up, you know, let him play. Ended up, the Cuban hired him to do solo at the restaurant. Last I heard, the son of a bitch started to learn Spanish so he could pass for a Cuban."

"And you were back where you started ... "

" ... Wearing a zarape vest and selling trinkets. Once more poised before the threshold of the Great Unknown."

"Fear and loathing," said Belinda, smiling.

Lennie took a last draught of his soft drink and pushed away from the table. Belinda touched up her make-up. He grabbed his notebook.

"Let's walk," said Lennie. "You feel like walking a while? Let's walk, come on."

"You don't mean, walk?" said Belinda, skeptically.

"Yeah, walk. You know, where you use your legs and feet and you sort of move from one place to another. I know Texans don't walk, but this is New York. In New York, you walk. Unless you take a cab. It's the law."

"Are you going to give me a tour of Greenwich Village?"

"Ain't much to see. You interested in seeing Edgar Allan Poe's house?"

"Does he still live there? Will he see us?"

"Not really. What I had in mind is going over to Washington Square. Watch the people. One of the best reasons to live in New York. There's no other place that has the people New York has."

"I see people all the time. I'm not much of a people watcher," Belinda said. "Say, don't you have to get back to work? What about free enterprise?"

"Rico doesn't mind. It's kind of slow this time of day. He likes to go home about six. If I don't get back by then, he'll be pissed. We got till six, how about it?"

"Okay. Sure. Let's go see the people."

Belinda picked up her tray and looked for a trash bin. Lennie gathered up his notebook under his arm and told Belinda to just leave the tray.

Outside of Blimpy's, the crowd of tourists and office workers had thinned. Belinda and Lennie had the entire block to themselves. Belinda indicated the sky with a flick of her head. It was hot, muggy and gray. They walked on Bleecker toward New York University.

"See that bar there?" said Lennie, "they say that in the bathroom, is where Edward Albee read the graffiti that said, "Who's Afraid of Virginia Woolf."

"Who's afraid of Edward Albee, I say."

They walked past Circle in the Square and on to the corner, across from the Bleecker Street Cinema. Belinda bought oranges from a sidewalk vendor. She handed one to Lennie.

"How long will you continue to be a writer of songs that nobody sings?"

"I don't know. Not too much longer, probably. It's been a long time since somebody told me I wrote good songs. It's pretty bad when even your friends stop being nice and polite to you. Tell you you write good songs. Sometimes I think I don't have it anymore."

"Sounds to me like you're just homesick," said Belinda, beginning to peel an orange.

"Maybe. How can you can tell?"

"I can tell," she said, coyly.

"Yeah, you could say I'm homesick, a little. I guess, you're right."

"I'm never away from home long enough to get homesick. What do you miss most? About home?"

"I don't know, exactly. I never think at all about Corpus. The only thing I can think of is the beach at Padre, and that isn't even in Corpus. You can stand on a sand dune on Padre Island and imagine no other human being has ever stood on exactly that spot. You turn to look out on the Gulf, and way out there, at a point where the water and the sky meet, if you just fix your eyes on that point, it seems like you're the only human being on earth. It's a kind of solitude that doesn't exist anywhere else on the planet."

"You mean, I can go out there and experience it, too," Belinda said.

"No, that's not what I mean at all. It has to do with a particular moment. There's a lot of things that have to come together at that precise moment. When it happens, it's like you feel this solitude come over you. It's scary, at first, because you've never felt anything like it before. You're the only living being in the universe."

"It sounds religious," said Belinda.

"It is, that's right, it is. It can only happen when you stand alone before the ocean, I think. When it happens, you begin to look for signs of it in other people, but you never see it. People equate solitude with death, and death is something to run away from. They spend their whole lives trying to avoid death."

"Do you blame people for that?"

"No, of course, not. Solitude isn't death. In fact, solitude is the only way to conquer death. The fear of it, anyway. We don't want to die because we don't want to leave anything behind, property, loved ones. On the other side is the unknown. Maybe there's an After-Life, maybe not. When you find your private moment of solitude, you get a tremendous sense of power over the world you live in."

"How so?"

"Well, for the first time, you begin to live. Food seems to taste better. People you know become more interesting. All because you've removed a barrier that separated you from the world. Everything prior to that was filtered through your own ego."

"I don't think it's happened to me, so far."

"It's different for everybody, the moment when it comes. I go to the beach out here, Coney Island, and I never get that same feeling. It can't be the sand, or the water, or the sky. For me, it has to be Padre Island."

"It'd never occur to me that they'd have a beach here."

"Sure, there is. It's not the same, though. There's Nathan's. That's the only thing from here that I would put on Padre Island. Nathan's hot dogs."

"If you put one on Padre, then it wouldn't be Nathan's."

"Naw, it probably'd be Raul's or Jorge's. Not Nathan's."

"And, it would be tacos, not hotdogs."

"I guess. What I'm trying to say is that you can be from only one place. You might leave and you might never get back to it, but it will always be the place where you're from."

"You are homesick!"


Lennie and Belinda came upon Washington Square Park, entering though a canyon of high-rise university dormitories. As they scanned the park for a likely place to sit, they saw that most of the people in the park were gathered in the center at the water fountain. Lennie indicated a grassy area to their left. They sat on a bench.

Belinda leaned over to feed tiny bits of orange peel to the pigeons that flocked to her feet. She stopped when she saw that they pecked at the ground but would not eat them. She placed the remainder of the peel on the bench beside her.

"All I ever wanted to do was get out of San Antonio. We had a porch in back of our house with a swing on it. I'd go there after supper and sit. I'd close my eyes and sit there. Sometimes I'd still be sitting there when my mother would come out to tell me it was bedtime. What I wanted, when I closed my eyes, was for a day or two to pass before I opened them again. The only thing keeping me in San Antonio was my age. If I were old enough, I thought, I could leave."

"What was so important about leaving?" said Lennie, vaguely amused.

"I can't tell you that because I don't know. I couldn't wait to get out, that's all. One day, there I was, on a bus going to Austin. My father, my brothers, my uncles, my cousins, my friends, everybody, all of them wanted to drive me to school. They couldn't see me going up there all by myself. I had a suitcase and a small box of books and some love letters from my boyfriend. I told everybody they would get a chance to bring me things as I needed them. I just couldn't let all those people, all of whom I loved, deprive me of my first experience of freedom, of being on my own."

"How was it ... the freedom?"

"Not what I thought it would be. It was mostly confusing. Later, when I got settled in and I felt safer, that's when I began to feel like I was finally free. Growing up I felt confined. I wanted to break out, to just go away. I made up my mind that I was never going to be confined. I had waited all my life to finish high school. From the first day I ever walked into elementary school, that's all I ever wanted to do. Just grow up, finish it, and be done with it. I had no idea what it would be like. I wasn't thinking of the future or what I would become. I just wanted out of school. It was the one thing that made me feel like a prisoner."

"But you went to school in Austin, right? Another prison?"

"It was supposed to be different, though. The way my cousins told me about it, it wasn't like high school. You had so much more freedom, they said. By then, I had something else to worry about."

"What was that?"

"It started the summer between high school and college. My mother wanted me to find a job for the summer to earn some of my own money for the fall. My father disagreed. He said money wasn't a problem, that I should read and prepare for college so I could get a leg up and be ahead of everybody else by the time the term started. My aunts and uncles, my married brothers and sisters, it seemed like they never left the house that summer. They all were telling me what I should do with my life."

"What about you? What did you want to do?" Lennie began to peel his orange, uncovering one wedge, eating it, uncovering another.

"Get away, get away from the suffocation. There was plenty of time to think about what to do with my life. Each one of them had an idea as to what I should do. I guess they figured that if they got to me early on, convinced me to follow their advice, then they could take credit for my life afterward. It got to the point where I don't think it mattered to them that it was my life. What mattered is what they had in mind for me."

"I think that when people get to be a certain age, they want to do things over. Make up for the past, choose the opportunities they should have taken. Go back to the fork in the road and check out the road not taken. If you had done what anyone of them wanted you to do, they probably wouldn't have liked you very much."

Lennie tossed a sliver of orange flesh to the pigeons, who fluttered their wings in panic.

"That's just it! I was so busy rejecting their suggestions that I began to worry about the things I was interested in. I mean, the only things I knew for sure boiled down to what I didn't want to do. I thought that if I just stood still, something was bound to happen. I mean, it's inevitable. That's how I wanted to live. Just let things happen."

"I think I understand. A little, anyway. I've always wanted to do something with music. Play piano, guitar; write songs. Even when I was a little kid. It's all I've ever wanted to do."

"Sure, it's easy when you have a talent like you do. It's like you really don't have a choice. You want to do it because you have the talent for it. Like you were meant to do it, so you don't mind that you don't get to choose. It's easy that way. I didn't have that kind of talent."

"It doesn't take much talent to live life," said Lennie.

"In the fall of that year, the first thing I discovered is that I didn't want to be in college. I didn't mind the studying part of it, I could always make good grades. It wasn't what I had in mind. I was miserable."

"Maybe you only thought you were miserable."

"What's the difference? Anyway, I interviewed for a job as a stewardess. The interviews were supposed to be for graduating seniors but I got interviewed anyway. I got a letter from Houston telling me I should stay in school, but that I had the job anytime I wanted it."

"I could have guessed you were a stewardess."

"But, you didn't."

"But, I didn't. I've only flown in an airplane twice in my life."

"I fly out of Houston. That's where I keep my apartment. I enrolled in the university there, to finish my degree. I can't help thinking how disappointed my parents will be if I don't."

"Are you flying now, stopping over in New York?"

"I have a very important decision to make. That's why I'm here. I was supposed to make it this morning, in fact. I couldn't bring myself to do it."

"Of all the places in the world you could fly to, you came to this very important postage stamp of concrete to make your decision."

"You can make fun of me, if you want. Talking to you is actually helping me to decide."

"Can I ask what this agonizing decision is all about?"

"It's not that bad, really. I mean, there's not much agony to it. It's my boy friend. He flew in from Houston this morning."

"You weren't there to meet him? Or, did you run out on him."

"I didn't run out on him. I couldn't stand to see him, that's all. If I went to the airport, he'd want my answer even before his luggage came out of the chute."

"He wants to know whether you're going to marry him or not."

"That's right."

"And, you want to marry him, but not right now. But, he has warned you. If you don't do it now, then you might not get a chance later."

"Something like that."

"In the meantime, he landed at the airport, you weren't there, and he's at your hotel right now. Waiting for you. Like Cookie and the Cupcakes used to sing, 'Wondering where you are, wondering why you had to go.'"

"I got into a panic this morning and I couldn't face him. I had to go off and be by myself."

"Think things over?"

"No, I've done too much of that. I just wanted not to think about it. Put it out of my mind for a few hours. I got hungry and went into Blimpy's to eat. Before that, I was feeling guilty, so I called in a message for my boyfriend. The desk clerk said he was in the room already, if I wanted to talk to him. I didn't feel like talking to him. Damned hotel clerk trying to run my life for me, too. I left a message for him, telling him not to worry."

"That was nice of you."

"That's the part that pisses me off the most. I feel that I have to do these things, all the time. I want to do things for myself and not worry about what it'll mean to somebody else. But I can't. All the time, I have to be responsible and I have to think about what I'm doing, or else somebody'll get hurt, or they'll be disappointed. No matter how hard I try, I always come back to doing what people expect of me."

"What's wrong with that? We're all responsible to somebody. If not to others, then to ourselves. It's the price we pay for civilization. 'No man is an island,' said the Reverend Donne."

"I feel as though I'm in a trap with the door open. I mean, the door is right there open for me to get out and I won't."

"Most people are grateful to have such traps. What you call a trap, other people call comfortable shoes, home and hearth, etc."

"Maybe so. I still wish I could live on an island."

"What good would that do?"

"On an island, there wouldn't be any people. I could just live and let things happen. Something comes up, I do it. I want to take things as they come."

"You're worried that your life up to now, along with the future that's about to kick you in the ass, will consist of doing things you don't want to do but that you have to do, else the people you love will be disappointed and you can handle being miserable better than they can handle being disappointed. Is that about right?"

"Who knows? All I know is, I don't have much of a choice."

"It's not choice that you want. If you genuinely had to choose, you'd go nuts. You want the semblance of choice."

"I really do want to choose. You don't understand."

"Let's say you really don't have to marry this guy. Or anybody. What say you and I run off to an island somewhere together."

"Where? Which one?"

"Doesn't matter. An island."

"Padre Island?"

"It's an island. Manhattan is also an island."

"And what? Get married, have kids? Trade him for another of the same?"

"No, who said marriage, kids. Not what I meant at all. That wouldn't be a choice, would it? We go somewhere. You feel trapped, you leave. That simple."

"What then? Where would I go?"

"Go to someone else. Or, to no one else. Whatever you want to do. Except, all you'll find is a series of connecting traps. No doors. You exit one, you enter another, and then another. It's called life."

"Not at all. You're wrong! There's got to be more. I just know it."

"Let me ask you something. Why are you marrying this guy? It seems obvious to me that you're going to marry him. Your mind is made up to do it."

"I don't have any reason not to marry him. He's very good to me. He doesn't have a lot of money right now, but he will, I mean, he has a future. I mean, there's all those reasons to marry. Even if I had a reason not to, or a lot of reasons not to, they probably wouldn't be enough. The reasons to marry him are overwhelming."

"Don't you think you ought to go with how you feel? How do you feel about it? Don't feelings count for something? Even if you can't say it, you can feel it and that's a way of knowing things."

"You mean, do I love him?"

"No, yes. Love is part of it, not all of it."

"I care for him, if that's what you mean."

"But, you're still missing something. Adventure, romance, excitement. All the things of youth?"

"Don't be cynical."

"Who's being cynical. Look, I came to New York to find fame and fortune. That quest was to be accompanied by adventure, romance, and excitement. What I found is an apartment that's got cockroaches and dust that's impossible to get rid of. Black dust that gets gummy and gooey. You walk out in the street wearing a white shirt, it turns gray by the time you get to the subway. I eat at Blimpy's because I don't have enough money to eat any place else. I don't eat in my apartment because I don't know how to cook, I don't want to cook, and I don't want to fight the roaches for my food. My bed is a mattress on the floor, I have a bathtub in my kitchen, and I have to take a crap in a stall down the hall. Adventure, romance, and excitement? If I'm having it, I sure would like someone to explain it to me. It's not what I thought it would be. In fact, sometimes I look forward to the day when I get the hell out of here just so one day I can look back fondly on all this. I have a feeling I'm having the time of my life and don't know it. There are too many trivial details for me to see it properly."

"That's where you and I are different."

"I don't think we're so different. I'm pretty sure I disappointed a lot of people when I came to live in New York. I know I'm disappointed in myself. Thing is, I'm here and I have to make the best of it."

"It's different for you. It's always different for men."

"Maybe so, but it doesn't have to be. Greenwich Village is the place for people to live outside of convention. A few months, a year, two years. Nobody stays. Once you sweat out your youth, you go back, lean and hungry, to where you came from."

"Full of Blimpy's sandwiches?"

"With a little wisdom, too."

"Listen," said Belinda, "there's too many people in the park here. Can we go to your place? You can play me one of your songs."

"I am told my songs have a great seductive power. Are you strong enough to resist? What will happen if you don't?"

"At this moment I think I want to find out. For myself."

"Oh, ye of frail resistance."

"You should be glad of that."

"What about your boyfriend?"

"I'll never see you again, so what's the harm?"

"I don't know what to think about that."

"You'll have someone to listen to your songs. I might tell you I like them. If I really like them, I might see you again. Who knows?"

"Be not afeard: the isle is full of noises, sounds and sweet airs that give delight, and hurt not."

# Bink's Waltz

The bartender sat on a rickety stool at the far end of the bar, where it was dark and cool. A neon beer sign cast an amber glow over his head. Walter Mendez came in and took a stool near the entrance. He removed his suit jacket, draping it over the backrest of the stool. His undershirt was sopping wet. The bartender looked in Walter's direction and turned away with a calculated indifference. He had an elbow planted on the bar, making a pedestal of his hand to rest his head on.

Walter Mendez spread both of his hands over his face to wipe away the sweat he brought in from the heat outside. The bartender brought his free hand up to his mouth. A cigarette was stuck between his ring and middle fingers. It took several attempts to find his lips before he enveloped the filtered tip. After drawing on the cigarette in a profound gesture of lassitude, he allowed his arm to float to his side. The bartender had not the energy, it seemed, to exhale. The smoke billowed out of his mouth in a white stream, following the contours of his face, curving over his forehead, then ballooning as a bulky cloud over his head.

Walter placed his own elbows on the bar, clasping his hands together in an attitude of prayer. It was a day that bespoke time, age, the emptiness of things. The bartender didn't seem to be in a hurry and neither was Walter.

The picture window to the left of Walter Mendez was painted in red up to a short man's shoulders. The sunlight of early afternoon made the paint glow. The filtered light cast a rusty dusk into the dim bar. Walter noticed the bristle traces left by the paintbrush where the paint had not been applied smoothly or thickly enough. In the rectangle of clear glass above the red screen, "Sally's" was written in an ornate black script, the work of a good sign painter.

"What kinda beer you want," the bartender said at last from his perch at the end of the bar. His voice was low, laden with life's fatigue and phlegm. He was relatively young, Walter's age. Thirty-five, Walter would guess. Less than forty, bottom line.

The bartender made no effort to move from his barstool. Walter figured him for a man who would calculate the effort it takes to get up on the stool and multiply it by the effort it would take to get back on it. It was not so much an economy of movement as it was a conservation of strength.

Beneath the apron of the bar, there was a long beer cooler divided into discrete compartments. It had seen better days. The brightwork of the humped sliding doors had been worn down to a mottled layer of chocolate rust. The beer cooler seemed to offer far too much storage for the number of people the small place could hold.

Walter Mendez called a Miller Lite. With great effort, the bartender slid off the barstool, twisting his body, giving the impression of a man dismounting from the saddle.

The bartender had a deformed, almost grotesque way of walking. One leg was shorter than the other. To compensate, the sole of his right shoe was three inches thick, with the heel yet an inch thicker. As he walked, he stooped forward, his hand on his thigh, to move his deformed leg in a wide arc in front of him. It was as if he were going into position on the line of scrimmage. He leaned over backwards to balance his weight before he moved his good leg.

The beer he sought was in a compartment directly in front of Walter Mendez. When the humped door was opened, the compressor motor began to roar as if to protest the disruption of its inactivity.

"It's quiet in here," said Walter Mendez, acting upon a sudden urge to hear a human voice.

"This time of day," said the bartender, with a shrug. He dipped deep into the cooler for Walter's beer. He winced and brought his palm to the side of his head. He held the beer in one hand, and leaned his weight on a shoulder against the bar and a hip against the cooler.

"Hard night?" asked Walter.

"Night was great," said the bartender. "Getting over it is what's not so fucking hot!"

A churchkey hung suspended on kite string tied to a corner of the beer cooler. The bartender took a moment or two before the pain in his head subsided sufficiently enough for him to master the complexities of uncapping the beer bottle.

Walter Mendez shook a last cigarette out of a crumpled package, tossing the empty package on the bar. He reached in his pocket for a throwaway lighter, which he threw on the bar without lighting the cigarette. He stuck the cigarette in his mouth, raised a haunch to pull out his wallet. Walter turned his head to one side, in the direction of the entrance. He noticed the cigarette machine, battered, with faded pictures of different cigarette brands. The price of cigarettes was scrawled on a piece of cardboard taped next to the coin slot. Six quarters.

"How often do they stock fresh cigarettes?" asked Walter.

"Hell, I don't know, mister," said the bartender.

The bartender dropped a frayed coaster in front of Walter and set the bottle of beer on top of it. The warped coaster was flattened by the weight of the beer bottle. The bartender placed his hands on the bar and leaned on them, his head bent low, shutting his eyes tightly. He waited for Walter to pull some money out of his wallet.

The bar was solidly constructed. Plywood, Walter guessed, two by fours, and formica for the top. There was a padded strip of naugahyde for the elbows of customers. The formica, warped where the precut pieces were tacked in place, was a magenta color with flecks of gold in it. A strip of aluminum ran the length of the bartender's side.

Walter Mendez took the first sip of the cold beer. The cold taste of it made him tremble. He grimaced and immediately took another sip. His eyes became glassy as he raised the bottle in a salute.

"First of the day," said Walter.


Sally's, except for Walter Mendez and the bartender, was empty. The front part of Sally's was long and narrow, hardly more than eight or ten feet across; most of which space was taken up by the bar. Further into the place, where the bar ended, demarcated by a gaudily-colored jukebox, was an open area, perhaps twenty-feet square.

Against the rear wall, directly in Walter's line of sight, were stacked cases of longneck empties. The remainder of the room was taken up by sturdy tubesteel and formica tables and vinyl-covered chairs, all in brown and black. Each table had a salt shaker and an ashtray on it.

Next to the cases stacked against the rear wall, Walter could see the door to the men's room, painted brightly red. Almost every inch of free wall space, beginning at the entrance, was decorated with beer posters. Little Joe for Schlitz, Laura Canales for Budweiser, a giant armadillo for Lone Star, and a Swedish-looking blue-eyed fellow holding up a Hamm's. The latter, it seemed to Walter, was strangely out of place.

The bartender took Walter's dollar and placed a quarter in change on the bar. Walter shoved the quarter back toward the bartender.

"You want to drop it in the jukebox," Walter said, flicking at the quarter with his fingernail.

"No. Shit, no!" said the bartender, without being surly, but with an expression full of dulled pain. "I like it quiet. You wanna play something, mister, it's up to you. Me, I kinda like it quiet, for now."

Walter said, "You want quiet. Strange line of work for a man who wants quiet." Walter upended the beer bottle once more.

The bartender shrugged as if he had blurted out too much of his business. He ran a hand, fingers spread out, through his hair. He then leaned forward, placing both hands on the bar, his palms overlapping the edge to support his weight.

"Hey, I had a hard night, mister. You know how it is. It's my head, my head don't feel so good. Feels like it's floating in a puddle of dog piss." He picked up the quarter and rolled it over his forefinger a couple of times.

"Look, you want me to play the jukebox, it's o.k. I play the jukebox. What kinda music you like? It's mostly Chicano music, you know. There's some shit from Mexico, I think. Not the mariachi, but those fuckers that try to sing like Frank Sinatra. They all, all those fuckers sound the same to me. Faggot-sounding motherfuckers!"

"Why not change the records?" said Walter. "Can't you get something else on there?"

"Sally has the jukebox man put them on there. Nobody but Sally ever plays them. Shit, he ain't even here half the fucking time. Me? I'd just as soon go with Frank Sinatra. Go with the real thing! There's some shitkickers in there. George Strait, Hank Williams, Jr. There's a group, Highway 101. That Paulette Carlson, man. Belts out a song so your chest hair curls at twenty paces. You don't look to me like you want to hear shitkicker, right?"

"No, no shitkickers," Walter said. "Come to think of it, maybe quiet is better. Whyn't you keep the quarter anyway."

"Nobody tips here," said the bartender, rolling the coin over his forefinger some more before slipping it into his pocket. "Anything you say, though."

"You feel that bad, why not let me buy you a beer," said Walter.

"Hair of the dog never did work for me, you know? What happens, I just get fucked up again. Never fails," said the bartender, sadly.

"You call it, then. It's right there, you feel like it," said Walter, placing another dollar bill on the bar.

"What the fuck!" sighed the bartender, drawing up the sliding door of the beer cooler. He jerked the cap and set the bottle on the bar.

"I have to leave the bottle sit there for a while, you know? I have to look at the son of a bitch. That way, I know exactly what I'm getting into. I used to try and figure out who's in charge, me or what's in that fucking bottle. Shit! Wasn't ever anything to figure, you know? I tell myself, one day, I'm gonna beat that son of a bitch. One day."

"You have a problem with it, I take it," said Walter, gently.

"Yeah," said the bartender, shaking his head. "Yeah, I got a fucking problem with it. You can say that."

Walter bought the bartender three more beers. The sunlight entering the bar became less intense as the afternoon waned. Walter'd had
two more himself. The carcass of a ten dollar bill lay on the bar. The
beers had done wonders for the bartender. The lines were gone from
his face, he was livelier; less lethargic. He was able to move his head,
talk, wave his arms, without grimacing in pain.

"What are you looking for, anyway? I think you're looking for something," the bartender said to Walter. The tone of voice breathed a question mark. He burped and his eyes watered. He brought the back of his
hand up to his mouth and burped again.

"You don't look to me like the type who'd come in here 'cause he
has to. That's all what's come in here. People with no other place to
go."

"Business. I'm in town on some business," said Walter.

"Over at the theater, with that culture group, hunh? You one of
them artist types?"

"No. Not an artist," said Walter, and let it go at that.

"Now. Let me see. What else could bring you here. You want drugs?
You one of those straight arrows hits the ski slopes on weekends? Score
some nose candy for yourself, that it? That what brings you here?"

"Nope," said Walter. "Not drugs."

"Fact is, I don't know nothing about drugs. Sally don't want them in
here. I see somebody on needlejuice, I throw the fucker out. Simple as
that. I got Sally's blessing on that. Out they go. Besides, the customers
here, there ain't nobody here right now, but when they're here, they're
mostly old, you understand. They don't take drugs. Shit's for the young,
anyway. Age takes care of anything these old guys need. To be frank
with you, it don't look to me like you take drugs."

"That's what I said, no drugs," said Walter.

"Women? We got women. Women we got. They might be one time
too many round the block, but we got them. You be here next couple
of hours, they'll be here. Looks to me like you could do better, though.
But, then, you never know, do you? You might like what's to offer here.
If your interests lie in that direction, it ain't too hard to take one of them
home, or wherever you might be bunking. I can tell you that much.

"That sounds a little more interesting," said Walter.

"They're not for hire, though, if that's what you think. I wouldn't
say they're in business. What they are, is, grateful. They're the most
grateful bunch I ever saw. Full of gratitude, they are. In fact, the more
you fill them up with wine coolers, the more grateful they get. See those
wine coolers back there on the counter? We sell them for two bucks a
pop. Women, they come in here, they drink that shit. Makes them
feel like ladies, I think. They suck down a couple of bottles there, and

they get goddamned elegant. They wiggle the little pinkie, just like that, when they get one of these old fuckers to buy'm one. All they do is get pretty damned drunk, seems to me. Elegant or no."

"I'd like to see that," Walter said.

"You gotta buy one of them a lot of wine coolers if you want to get her home with you. I expect you gotta do your business real quick, fuck her, that is, else she probly'll nod out on you before you can shake a piece loose."

"I don't think so," Walter said.

"So, that's all there is, around here. We got basic brew and basic broads. Now, you know everything I know."

Walter Mendez made a quick trip to the bathroom. The bartender was now sprightly and quick in his movements. Walter was beginning to feel lightheaded. He was unaccustomed to drinking so many beers at one sitting.

"I'm actually looking for somebody. An old man. I've been trying to track him down. Every time I'm in town, if there's nothing else for me to do, I look for him a couple of hours. Stop at a place like this, ask a question or two. And, then, I'm on my way. I don't really expect to ever find him. I did at first, but not anymore. I look anyway. Gives me something to tell the folks when I get back home. Give them a little report. Makes them feel better."

"I thought so. You never did look like a tourist. Where are you from?"

"Brownsville."

"Oh, yeah? Brownsville. Sure, I heard of it. Where is it?"

"On the border. Far south as you can go," said Walter. He tapped the bottom of the beer bottle on the bar, signalling for another.

"Yeah, that's right. On the border. So, you're from Brownsville on the border. What about this old man you're looking for? What'd he do?"

"I didn't say he did anything. The family's been looking for him. He might be a relative, that's all."

"Your family. Is that like your mother and father?"

"More like brothers and sisters."

"Could this fellow be your father, if I was to ask and you were to say?"

"He might. I can't say because I don't know. That is, I'm not sure. There's not much about him that we're sure of. Not much at all."

"What happens when you find him?"

"I don't know what happens. I don't think I'll ever find him. I've never given thought to what I would do if I were to find him. Maybe looking for him is what's important, not finding him. That's what it seems like, sometimes."

"I don't get it, mister," said the bartender.

"Skip it, doesn't matter," said Walter.

"Now, wait a minute. You say you've been searching for this old man for a long time, just to sort of look him up?"

"All I do is look for him, that's all. At first, I probably thought I could find him. Seemed easy. We're pretty sure he's here, that he lives here in San Antonio."

"San Antonio's a big city. It ain't as big as most people think it is, but it's big," said the bartender.

"Yeah, it's a big city, alright. It's a city split up into different parts. I know he might be in this neighborhood and not in that one. So, I say to myself, where could he be that I couldn't track him down."

"You some kind of detective?"

"No. It's a process of elimination, that's all. You narrow it down and then you narrow it down some more and after you narrow it enough, that's where he has to be. Shouldn't be much to it. That's what I thought, anyway"

"You ain't never been able to turn him up?"

"Well, yeah, I turned him up, alright. I narrow it down to where he's supposed to be and when I get there he disappears. I have to start the process of elimination all over again."

"Sounds to me, mister, like this fellow don't want to get found."

"That's right. I get close enough and he moves on. It's become a little game between us. He stays just a little ahead of me so that I have to keep looking. After a while, I got used to just looking. Going through the motions."

"How come? I mean, why is it so important?"

"My family, sisters and brothers, they expect it of me. That's why I keep doing it."

"What if they said you don't have to look anymore?"

"I never gave it a thought, what it would be like if I didn't have to look for him."

"I'd like to help you, if I can," said the bartender. "How about a picture? You got a picture of him or something. I could pick him out if you gotta picture. I know most every face that comes in here. Tell you what time they get here."

"No, there's no picture of him."

"How about you describe him. You know what he looks like? Is he got a scar, or something? Something'll make it easy to pick him out?"

"No. I don't even know what he looks like."

"Hey, that's a hell of thing, mister," said the bartender, picking out another beer from the cooler. Walter pushed a dollar bill toward him.

"That is one hell of a thing," continued the bartender. "Your family, you say, sends you to look for this fella. You don't know who he is or what he looks like. Am I getting close?"

"It's not quite like that," Walter said.

"Well, let me ask you this. Could it be that you already met this dude, somewhere, you know, looked him right in the eye and, could it be, you didn't even know he was the one you're looking for? Could it be something like that?" The bartender spoke impatiently, the beer he'd been drinking slurring his speech.

"No. No, it couldn't. I'd know him if I saw him."

"It's not like that bullshit thing about New York, is it? I told this fucker, once, I says I was in New York for a coupla days and he says, did you happen to run into my cousin, he lives there. There's nine million people, nine fucking million people, that live in New York City. Imagine me running into this fucker's cousin inna middle of nine million fucking people?"

"It's not like that," said Walter.

"What about a name? You can track people down if you got names for them."

"Wouldn't help. Every time I get close to him, he moves on and I have a suspicion that he changes his name. He knows I'm looking for him and he doesn't want to be found. He moves on, leaving just enough of a trace so he doesn't disappear completely. Takes me a while, but I get on to him again."

"What does that tell you?"

"He doesn't want to be found, but he doesn't want me to stop looking."

"Well, how about this? He knows you're looking for him. My guess is he could find you if he had a mind to. Right? He lets you find him, at least, he lets you get close enough to know he's o.k. I'd say, why bother more'n that? Seems like he's told you all he wants you to know. He's saying to you, I'm o.k, now, leave me the fuck alone."

"It's not that simple. I wish it were that simple."

"You got me, mister. How about another beer?"

"Sure, in a minute."

The door to Sally's opened to let in a wide swath of bright sunlight. A flush of heat and noise swept in with it. It was as if the roar of a waterfall had been suddenly triggered. Walter became annoyed that whoever it was coming in kept the door open. He thought it might be someone checking the ambiance before committing to walk in fully.

Walter looked to his left, over his shoulder, in the direction of the entrance. He saw an old man, dressed in a black suit, making a laborious effort to walk inside. The old man carried a walking cane hooked over his forearm. He moved artificially erect, a created posture that seemed habitual, practiced and perfected over the years. In small, measured half-steps that scraped the floor he made his way inside.

After the old man cleared the swing path of the door, he turned around to face the street again. He retraced his steps, moving toward the door to close it. He slammed the door shut with a bit more force than was necessary. The old man slid the cane into one hand and with the other, fingers extended, he smoothed his shirt front and then he touched the knot of his tie. All of his preparations completed, he turned to walk purposefully in to the bar.

Walter turned away from the old man to upend his beer bottle. Behind Walter came the tattoo of the cane on the floor. It wasn't quite the tap of a blind man feeling his way forward. And neither was it the isolated tap of someone using the cane for support. The cane was an affectation and a precaution, a just-in-case object. The tapping of the cane came in counterpoint to the shuffle of the old man's feet on the floor.

"Bink," said the bartender, as the old man reached the end of the bar, "now, he might be the kinda guy you're looking for."

The bartender shifted his weight to his good leg, going into the cooler for a bottle of Pearl. He held up the bottle for Walter to inspect.

"Makes you wonder," he said. "According to news reports, you got Budweiser and Miller. Big sellers. In here, though, my customers stick to Pearl, Lone Star, Falstaff. Some old guy even keeps asking me to put Jax in the cooler. Imagine that. Fucking Jax!"

Walter took another sip of his Miller Lite.

The old man, Bink, stopped at the end of the bar. He surveyed the open area, the tables and chairs, as if to ascertain the availability of his usual place. He had some distance to walk yet. The bartender, beer in hand, his own walk slowed by his deformity, went to the end of the bar to wait for the old man to sit.

When the old man sat, but was not yet comfortably settled, the hovering bartender set the bottle on a coaster after which he made his way back behind the bar. He took a Big Chief tablet from under the bar and wrote in it.

"My customers go a long way on ceremony," said the bartender by way of explanation when he returned to his place in front of Walter. He saw that Walter was curious about the Big Chief tablet and explained.

"Bink, he pays with his pension check. Or, social security. One of them, or maybe both. He keeps a tab that he pays every month, anyway. We don't do that as a rule, just for him. I started working here, three four years ago, Sally says put everything he wants on his tab. Wait till the first of the month and Bink will clear the tab. Been like that, every month, regular as anything.

"I'll tell you something else. Bink don't squawk about his tab. You tell him it's sixty-something dollars, and he puts three twenties and change on the bar. Just like that. Always carries exact change, too. It's like he knows, to the penny, what he owes. He never questions the tab here. He pays it just like it's called.

"I worked other places where people ran a tab till they was ready to leave for the night. You can't make some fuckers believe they drank that much. It's different, you know. You get a beer, you pull out a dollar. You call for a round, it's two, three, four bucks. You put your good time on a tab, it adds up. They act like you padded the tab, you know, make a little something for yourself. Shit! I wanna do that, there's ways to do it. Better to take the money each round, I say. Keeps everybody straight.

"Bink, now, Bink is different. I didn't wanna carry no fucking tab for him. Or, anybody. Tabs is trouble, just like I said. I try to explain to him, at first. You know, when I didn't hardly know him at all, how things are with me. Tabs is fucking trouble.

"Bink, now, Bink just holds up his hand, like he's trying to stop traffic. He don't wanna fucking hear it. It's like he's got rights, you know. I just got here and what the fuck do I know.

"That much of it was true. I didn't know dink. Not about Bink, anyway. Bink's kinda special around here. I'll tell you, I found that out real quick. Ain't too many around like him anymore, anywhere."

The bartender showed Walter the browned sheets of the Big Chief tablet. There were four columns on each page, each column headed by a month and year. Beneath each column was a number for the day, and beside it were stick numbers. In the latter pages, almost every entry was III.

"See! Goes back ten years!" There was pride in his voice.

"Bink, now, Bink there," said the bartender, "he drinks three beers, see, and he goes home. Hard to say what he does, exactly. When he goes home, I mean. Or wherever he goes. I don't think anybody knows what he does. Other than what you see of him here, nobody knows."

Once again, Walter Mendez felt the urge to go to the bathroom. He slid off the barstool.

"Hold on to that thought," he said, "I'll be right back."

When he returned, the bartender began again.

"That's the thing about Sally's, you know. All the life anybody has begins at the door and it ends at the door.

"It's funny, you know. About Bink, I mean. I been here now three, four years already. When I came on, Bink, well, he sort of came with the place. You know how it is. You ever done any barkeeping? You go work inna place and there's a buncha guys who think they have the run of the joint just because they been drinking there longer'n you been serving drinks there. They figure they got rights. Kinda guys end up being a lot of trouble. Kinda guys, sooner than later, think they got the right to decide who drinks in the place and who don't. You gotta set those kinda guys straight right away. Sometimes, the owner'll go along with them on account of they're his pals. So, you do the owner a favor, you know. Let those fucks know how things stand. Easy, like. Don't want the owner pissed off.

"Me, I can respect long time customers. They're what keeps a place in business. Over the long haul. I know the boss don't like to see long time customers, his friends, maybe, run off. Can't make them feel unwelcome, even if they act like assholes. Don't get me wrong. I got respect for them. I can even take shit from them, no sense in pissing off the boss, or anybody, you know.

"Bink was drinking here even before Sally bought the place. Sally's been here ten, maybe, going on eleven years now. Your relative, by the way, if he was here anytime ago, Bink'd know. You had a name, or something to go on, Bink'd be the one to talk to.

"Stories Sally tells, Bink used to get into it with the best of them. Long ago. Knew them all. Sally says a heart attack knocked ol' Bink on his ass, four, six years ago. Doctor ordered him to drink a glass of wine every day, be good for him. Bink hates wine, so he figures three beers is equal to a glass of wine. I doubt if he even talked it over with the doc. He just does it, you know. Goes his own way. Don't seem to bother him any."

Bink sat rock rigid in his chair. He had his head tilted in the way a bird does when listening for something. He stared at a point somewhere between the bar and the wall behind Walter. His arms lay straight out on the table, with the bottle of Pearl in the middle.

At a measured pace, Bink took small, delicate sips from the bottle. He held it high in the air, as if examining it, before tipping it over to lightly brush against his mouth. Bink sat as though he knew but did not care that he was being watched.

"Does he always sit that way?" Walter asked.

"Yep. I'll tell you something else, too. If I don't bring him another beer, he don't ask for one. I get busy sometimes, sort of lose track of him in the rush, you know? Ol' Bink won't say a word. He'll just sit there not even moving until I hurry on up and take him another beer. He never goes to the bathroom, either. Holds his leak until he gets to wherever it is he goes. He just sits there, just like you see him. Then, it gets time for him to play the jukebox."

"What's an old man like that play the jukebox for?" asked Walter.

"Well, now that you ask, there's a lot of them old farts like that. Play the jukebox, I mean. Old songs, mostly. Sally has them on there for them. Most of them'll play a ranchera, you know, with accordions or mariachis. Can't stand the shit, myself. Anyway, it's a sign that they're drunk already.

"You'd be surprised. A man sucks down half a dozen Lone Stars, or some other kinda horsepiss. You can almost see the years will peel off him. I won't say it makes them feel young again. I don't know about that. I do know, it makes them fucking forget how old they are.

"That's when they get pretty fucking patriotic. Fuckers'll throw back and yell so's the skin on the back of your neck crawls. I don't mean that they get proud to be Mexicans and they all of a sudden realize that the United States sucks. It's like each one of them is his own country. It's like a challenge to whoever don't like it. Get up, motherfucker and we'll settle it right here.

"Shit, mister, by the time they get to yelling, most of them, they can't even walk to the fucking bathroom, much less throw a punch. Some of'em'll piss their fucking pants, sometime or other, right where they sit. But that beer and them songs sure does it for them. That much you can see, you stick here long enough."

"What about Bink, there?" asked Walter. "He one of the patriots?"

"Bink? Naw. Not old Bink. No, sir. There usually ain't nobody here when he comes in. Way I see it, it ain't no point to yelling like they do if there ain't no one around who'll stand up to the challenge. They get like banty roosters. It's like they're strutting their stuff, except they're too old and too fucking drunk to get up from their chairs to do it. The yell does it for them. I figure it's a substitute for the hard-ons they can't get anymore.

"There was some guys in here, once, from California. They were doing something at that cultural theater, up the street. Gritos, the yells, have a purpose, they said. Explained it all to me, like I give a fat fuck, or something. Like I ain't got to keep an eye on those old fuckers so's the yelling is all they do.

"Sally don't like those people. Over at the cultural theater. Can't say I got much use for them, either. That group that came in from California? They know everything there is to know about Mexicans. They can't speak a lick of Spanish, but they know every fucking thing. About Mexicans and anything else. They ain't shy, either, 'bout letting you know it, too.

"They were gonna have a parade for the 16th of September. That'd be the grito that started it all, right? That meant they had to close the street. Hell, I don't give a fuck whether they have a parade or not.

"Except, Sally got all pissed off about it. Sally's got this thing where, when he's pissed off, everybody around him gets to be miserable. Sally don't like it 'less everybody's miserable. Said something about how it was gonna cut into his business. Sally ain't got no fucking business time a day they put on that parade, you understand?

"Thing is, Sally gets pissed regular about something or other. Don't matter much what it is. That's probably the point. Get pissed and it don't matter much what it is. After he's got everybody miserable and pissed off, he's fucking happy. Like a little fucking kid, he gets. I guess you've met a few like Sally yourself. Sure, you have, everybody has.

"Anyway, these fellas from California say that when Mexicans want to be free, they yell. One yells and that reminds some other fucker of his own situation and pretty soon, all of them are yelling. Way I figure it, if there's enough Mexicans yelling at the same time, you probably call it a revolution.

"Now, ol' Bink there, Bink don't yell. Never seen him do it. Just looking at him, the way he holds his head, like when he's sitting down over there, you know? Well, you just know he's done his share, and maybe more. There ain't nothing he's got to prove to anyone, anymore. I wouldn't say that he's done it all, but, I figure he's satisfied with what he's done.

"I get to be old, ol' Bink ain't a bad way to be."


"There's been people, the time I been here, who tried to talk to ol' Bink there. Bink, Bink sure don't talk. Not to anybody. What he does, he looks away from you, like he's telling you to go the fuck away. So you start to talk and you get the feeling that Bink is listening. When you're done talking, you wait. Then, you wait some more. You cough, or something. Let him know you expect an answer. This is it. Ol' Bink'll turn around, look you right in the eye, and then he turns away. Goes back to staring at the same spot that he stares at all the time.

"There's this old whore, as I remember, came in here one time. Time a day about like now. That was when I just started here. Before Sally chewed me out, telling me not to allow any whores in here.

"I asked Sally, flat out, how the fuck you tell what's a whore and what ain't. Sally said, you smell them. Well, that was one fucking tight-ass answer, 'sfar as I was concerned. So, I said, smell which part? Don't matter, says Sally, any part'll do. You can put your nose up their pussy, you want to, says Sally.

"Well, I never did find out how to tell a whore from somebody what gives it a-fucking-way. Maybe there's a difference. Shit, I don't know. I got to where I can spot those that'll cause trouble. Sally don't want no trouble, not with the cops, you know? Sally's scared shitless when it comes to cops.

"Anyway, this old whore comes in and just sits there, end of the bar. Ain't nobody in the place but Bink'n me. After a while, she says she needs some money to buy some milk for her kid. I thought she was putting the bite on me. It looked to me like she was too damned old to be feeding milk to any kid. Maybe she just said milk and she meant something else for somebody what's maybe not a kid anymore. What the fuck do I know?

"I play along, though. I said, shit, my own kids need milk and I ain't got no money for them, either. I work two jobs, I tell her. So, she gives me a sassy look for my trouble. Says she meant the gentleman, meaning Bink. She had him figured for a sport, maybe one could do with a early evening quickie.

"I didn't have to smell any part of her to know what she was up to. I shoulda told her to leave right then, you know. Only, it was early, not much doing. I figured, what kinda fucking trouble can she cause. Just me and ol' Bink in the place.

"She ain't paid for her beer yet. She sashays her ass, a big one, too, over in Bink's direction. Like she's out for a stroll, taking in the time a day. She leaves her purse on the bar like I can be trusted with it.

"I can tell, while she's going over to Bink, that she's undone one button, maybe two maybe more, on her blouse. Give Bink a good solid look at what she's got. What he can have, if he's a mind to want some.

"She sits with her back to me. She's got a hand on his arm already soon's she sits down. I get to thinking, maybe it's not such a good idea. Let her stay, I mean. Her blouse is hanging out, sides of her arms, so I figure she's got her titties hanging out for ol' Bink. She's desperate, so she's not gonna waste too much time.

"I figure, too, that it's time to take another beer out to the old man. Only, if I go over there and see what I know I'm going to see, I'm gonna have to put a stop to it. Who knows, I think to myself. Maybe the old man ain't in it for buying, but, what the hell, he can stand to get a good look. Anybody appreciates a look anytime. Probably a long time since he's seen a real pair of them. Maybe it's been years since he's had a chance at the real thing. So, I'm thinking, I can't do that to him. I can't put the kibosh on the old man.

"The old whore ain't much of a looker, you get a good look at her, up close. She's got this gut that sticks out like she's permanently knocked up. Sway-backed, too. We get a lot of them in here that's sway-backed. I say to myself, what the shit, titties is titties.

"So, I hold back on taking him his beer, which was gonna be his last anyway. Then, I thought I might have it all wrong, you know? It might just be that ol' Bink'll do alright for himself. There's nothing says an old man can't get it up and do right for himself.

"Up here, enda the bar's not close enough to make out what she was saying to him. Ol' Bink, I figure, is busy with himself, like he usually is. Not saying shit. I could hear that she was talking. Bink was staring as he usually does at a spot right there just behind your head. It didn't look like he was saying shit to her.

"I see her sucking on her beer every now and then and when she's not doing that, she's talking her head off to Bink. Then, this old whore, I swear, man, she leans over, kinda to one side, you know, so I won't see what's going on. She starts rubbing ol' Bink's dick. Zips it down and she's got her hand inside Bink's pants.

"It ain't the cops that I'm afraid of. Or, the liquor control boys. There ain't a cop in the world that'll bust a concrete princess 'cause she's pulled a titty out, if you know what I mean. Or, even she's got her hand in your crotch. No, sir. They bust them out inna street, where they hold up traffic.

"What I'm scared of, I'm scared Sally'll walk in. Sally's gonna bust my ass if he comes in and sees what's going on. That's what I figure. Sally sure goes on about those girls, you know. Them old girls don't hurt nothing. Never have. But, ol' Sally, he's got a thing about them.

"The old whore, well, she had her hand on old Bink's dork. I ain't saying she had his dick out for all the world to look at. I ain't saying that. I am saying, she was working on it good and proper, kinda rocking back and forth, kinda keeping up a good time for him.

"I figure I got to stop her. Kinda let her know that she's going too far. Doing her business right in here and I'm standing behind the bar, it ain't right. It's broad fucking daylight. Anybody can come in. Except, I'm just thinking I need to get over there and stop it. Only, I don't.

"We all gotta make a living, the way I see it. She had this look in her eye, when she came in. Her face, her face had a kiss-my-ass look to it. Like she thought she might be something hot. Maybe she was, twenty fucking years ago! She was too desperate. I figure, let her have her way and there's no trouble. Except, maybe for Sally walking in. Thing is, I believed the part where she said she needed quick cash for her kids. Maybe it wasn't her kids, exactly. Maybe it was her old man needed a little something for his bones. Kids, her old man, who knows, it's all the same. She was desperate to have that cash. She probably had a good ass-kicking waiting for her if she didn't come back with it. Being desperate and all, I got scared that she might just go down on him right where they sat. Give him a knob-job right over there, and there was not a damned thing I could do about it. I thought she might assume the position at any time.

"Only thing I can figure to do is take ol' Bink his third and last beer of the day. Only way I know to throw myself into it, even though it ain't none of my business what they do, except it is my business they do it in here.

"Thing is, I gotta do it so she don't get pissed off. I make a lot of noise when I walk and that was enough. When she heard me coming, she stuffed herself back in her clothes and brought her hand back up on the table. I took him his beer and left it there for him. Came on back here to the bar to mind as much of my own business as I could.

"Ol' Bink, now, he puts some bills on the table. Might be ones, fives, too far for me to see. The old whore keeps looking at him, shaking the money in her fist. Ol' Bink, he's back to looking at that space on the wall where he always looks. It's all over and she knows it. She sashayed back up to where I stood. Came back for her purse. She'd wadded up the money. Threw it into the purse like she was punching it or something. I kinda felt sorry for her. She looked at me like she wanted me to say something, anything, so she'd have an excuse to let go at me. Maybe she thought with a little more time, she'd've got the job done on him. It meant more bucks to her. So, I guess, she blamed me for it. She didn't get as much as she thought she was going to get.

"I told her the beer was on the house, she told me to get fucked. Nasty like.

"Soon after the old whore left that one time, Bink finished his beer and went home himself. It was like nothing ever happened. As usual, no goodbye, no wave, no I'll be back, no see you, no thanks, no nothing. Most people who come in here are never so drunk that they don't at least wave as they go out. Some of them are concentrating so hard on staying upright that when they break their concentration to wave, they just about fall right on the fucking floor. But, not ol' Bink.

"Near's I figure it, ol' Bink is probably a lot like the old man you're looking for."

The bartender had interrupted his conversation to walk over and serve Bink. The beers which he and Walter drank were conveniently at hand. Walter was on his fifth beer, and for a change, his body felt light and bearable, unobtrusively pleasant.

The old man had finished all three of his usual beers, but he continued to sit at the table, still staring at a spot on the wall just behind

Walter Mendez. Walter and the bartender took a moment to be quiet.

At last, they heard the rumble of the chair on the floor as Bink prepared to stand up. He leaned forward a little to push the chair away from the table. Once he cleared some space between table and chair, he sat straight up and became rigid as if he were a military school cadet. He spread his hands over each knee. As he got his bearings, he got on his feet, stiff, steady as a rock.

It was when he began to move forward that Bink betrayed his unsteadiness. There was a slight, almost imperceptible, waver. Each step was tentative in the way of someone attempting to walk in the dark in an unfamiliar room. He was wary of reflexes that were not what they used to be. Nevertheless, as he moved, there was nothing to indicate he wasn't in control of his movements. Bink was prudent, cautious.

As he watched him, Walter had the impression that Bink overcompensated for his age and for the beer he'd consumed. The bartender had read Bink correctly. The cautiousness incumbent with his old age did not seem to have come easy to him. The cane tapped on the floor as he moved.

Bink moved zigzagged between the chairs and tables until he got to the jukebox, where he stopped with an air of uncertainty, as if he were trying to recall something. He turned and slid a slow, but steady hand into his pants pocket. He retrieved a coin and dropped it in the coin slot of the jukebox. Without reading the selections available, he punched three buttons.

The lights on the box began flashing with an almost human exuberance, as if the machine had been eager and raring to go. The jukebox thundered to life with a hissing and a scratching noise. The volume was set from the night before, much too loud for the afternoon solitude of Sally's. The bartender had a remote switch behind the bar which he used to lower the volume to something tolerable.

As the tune began on the jukebox, it was not what Walter expected as a bar room song. The opening bars of it seemed to be played on an out-of-tune piano. There was a lugubrious, mournful quality to the melody, made more dream-like by the syncopated waltz time.

"What the hell kind of music is that?" Walter asked the bartender.

"Ragtime," he said. "I didn't know what the fuck it was, first time I heard it myself."

"Sounds like a waltz," I said.

"That's right. It's a ragtime waltz."

"Are they kidding with that instrument. Is it supposed to sound like that? What the hell kind of instrument is that?"

"It's a harpsichord," said the bartender. "Looks like a piano, but it ain't. That's the way it's supposed to sound."

"Never head of any such thing. How come you know so much about it."

"I don't. I don't know shit about it. Sally, though, he knows. Sally knows all kinda shit like that. Like, that record is called, 'Bink's Waltz.' Scott Joplin wrote it."

"Never heard of him either," said Walter, shaking his head.

"Sure you have, I bet you have," said the bartender. "Remember a movie with Paul Newman, remember where they're gonna get revenge on this guy, remember how they set up like phony bookmakers? You didn't see it? I think it was Ernest Borgnine who was the bad guy, played a mean bastard. What the hell was the name a that flick? Steve McQueen was in it, too. Took place inna Depression, you know, they wore these funny suits and shit. Well, the music they used in the movie was by Scott Joplin, see?"

"I don't go to movies much," said Walter.

"The guy that had this place before Sally probably liked that music. It was real popular for a while. I worked inna place, about the time the movie came out, had all kinda shit music from it. Sure you don't remember the name of that movie? Anyway, when Sally got the bar, the jukebox came with it. Alla records in it.

"There's a guy from the jukebox company comes in here once in a while. He's got what everybody wants to hear in the back of his station wagon. Cleans the machine, changes records on it. Sometimes he sits down for a beer. Tells me what records nobody plays anymore. Like I give a shit. Coupla times, maybe, Sally tells me to ask the guy to bring something that he wants on there. I bet every record is different from when Sally got the box. Except, for 'Bink's Waltz.' Sally keeps it on there for the old man, Bink."

"The name of the record is 'Bink's Waltz.' You're telling me this Scott Joplin guy wrote that record for the old man there?" Walter said. "I find that hard to believe."

"What are you talking about, mister?" said the bartender.

"The old man's name is Bink, right? What the hell else am I supposed to think. This Scott Joplin knows the old man, he writes a song for him, right? Isn't that what I'm supposed to think?"

"I don't know what you're supposed to think. But, I do believe you got it all wrong there. The old man's name ain't really Bink. At least, I don't think so."

Walter was on his sixth beer. He could feel the signals telling him he'd better quit soon, get something to eat.

"You said, if I remember correctly, that the man's name is Bink. When the old man came in. You called him, Bink. If that is not his name, you still called him Bink anyway."

"I only know the guy as Bink on account of Sally calls him Bink. Now that I think of it, Sally probably calls him Bink on account of that record. Ain't no other way to figure it.

"There's lot of people come in here, they get nicknames like that. There's a guy we call, 'Chimuelo,' 'cause he's missing his front teeth. He had these two teeth that went in there, where the old ones used to be, false teeth. Held them together with wire, or some shit. I don't know. He gets drunk one night and he's taking a leak and I guess he's fucking with them because he drops them in the pisser.

"Somebody'd taken a dump in there before he went in and didn't flush. So Chimuelo, who wasn't called that just then, looks at his two teeth at the bottom of the bowl and these turds is floating in the water. He gave up on those teeth right then and there.

"His friends that he drank with told him to go on and fish them out. Take them home and boil'em in water so the shit and germs and whatnot get killed. Somebody else told him to soak'em in alcohol, like for about a year at least.

"Then, his friends started to get rowdy. Anybody coulda seen it coming. Somebody said, be sure and scrape between the teeth, you never know what gets stuck in there. Then, somebody else said Chimuelo was gonna be talking real shit from then on.

"Well, I don't think any of what they were saying made any difference to Chimuelo. It was the thought that his teeth fell in with floating turds that got to him. No way he was gonna go near those teeth again.

"We had this old guy—he finally died—that came in to sweep the floors and scrub the shitters. Afterward, he'd stick around and drink whatever Sally paid him every night. He had this black rubber glove that he used to scrub the toilets. He pulled Chimuelo's teeth for him out of the commode. Didn't bother him any to do it. He had his rubber glove and that made everything okay.

"So, he goes in there and brings Chimuelo's teeth out and tries to give'm to him. Chimuelo wasn't gonna touch the motherfuckers. The swamper tries to give them over to Sally and Sally ain't about to touch the motherfuckers, either. Says he should give them to me. I ain't about to touch the motherfuckers, no fucking way. So, I wrap them in a bar rag.

"Sally tries again to give them to Chimuelo, all wrapped up, nice and neat. Except, Chimuelo ain't taking them. Not even wrapped in the bar rag. Sally tries to tell him that it costs a lotta damned money to get new teeth. Chimuelo don't give a shit. Those teeth ain't going in his mouth ever again.

"Sally gives them back to me, like I know what the fuck to do with them, right? I put them on the shelf, under the bar. They were there a long damned time. They're gone now, though. I don't know what happened to them. I guess Sally finally threw them out.

"Chimuelo never could afford again to get a new set of teeth. That's when everybody started calling him, Chimuelo, 'cause of his missing front teeth. Made these teeth, right here, see? look like fangs. I thought Vampiro would be a better nickname, but there's already somebody that has that one.

"There's hardly a Christian name used in this place, come to think of it, you know? People just say to each other, usted, or señor, real formal like. Sometimes, compadre, except you never know if they're real compadres or they just say that. Some of the old chucos still say, bato or ese. Mostly, though, they use the nicknames they pick up. Some probably have the same nickname from when they was kids.

"Bink's a name pinned on the old man long before Sally got this place. Nobody that I know of has ever tried to find out what his real name is. Maybe some of the old timers, back when he drank in the evening, maybe they know.

"You know, if he was to drop over dead right now, I wouldn't know what to tell the cops, you know, 'bout who he is, where he lives. That's just something nobody around here needs to know. People give out just what they need to get along, if you understand. You can figure he lives somewhere around here. In the neighborhood. Most of them do, come in here. Where exactly, nobody needs to know that. Nobody asks, nobody tells. Like I say, there's probably some old timers who'd know. They're always talking about how times were different. You and I probably will too, we get to be their age."

The record was ending. The music was hardly audible above the scratchy hiss. In the time the bartender was talking, Bink was turning, slowly and methodically it seemed, around and around. He remained stiff and erect, maintaining an exaggerated pose of dignity. As the last bars of the record played, Bink raised his left arm in the air. The crook of his cane hooked in the curve of his elbow. He brought up his right hand, pressing it against his ribcage. He tilted his head slightly, as if it were pressed against the cheek of an unseen woman.

The jukebox began to whirr and groan as it retrieved the expended record back into its storage slot. Bink approached the jukebox and punched the same numbers as before. A couple of seconds later, the record started to play again.

"He gets two plays for his quarter," said the bartender, looking in Bink's direction. "He used to punch up both numbers and got them to play, one right after the other. This new box is a cheater. If you punch up a song that's already stacked up to play, it'll just play it once and cheat you outta your next play. Old Bink figured that one out. Now, he waits until the record is over before he punches it up again."

As before, the old man Bink began a slow turn, arm in the air, hand on his ribcage, his cheek against the cheek of his invisible partner. There was a dreamy, sleeplike expression on his face.

"He always do that?" Walter asked.

"Long's I've been here," said the bartender.

The bartender and Walter Mendez remained silent as Bink danced, waltzed, and spun delicately, gracefully, in time with the music. His measured movements were more animated, drawn from the lethargy of age into perfect coordination with the waltz time. There was a light, breezy quickness to his step.

When the record ended, Bink stood still for a moment. He drew himself up, stretching to his full height, and bowed. Afterward, he patted down the skirt of his suitjacket, shot his cuffs, one after the other, the cane dangling in the crook of his arm. He glanced at his shoes. He gave a little twist to the knot of his necktie.

Bink's afternoon was over. He began his slow shuffling walk to the door. The spriteliness to his movements was gone. He pulled on the doorknob, shuffling backwards to open it. As the door opened, the dim interior of Sally's gradually became flooded with sunlight.

"Here," said Walter Mendez, shoving some bills toward the bartender. "I've had all I can take for an afternoon. You have a couple of beers on me when you feel like it."

"You know what they say, it ain't dying. It's the fear of living."

"You mean that old man?" said Walter.

"Naw," said the bartender. "I mean hangovers, man."

ACZ 3009                    2/20/96
    PS
    3563
    A73344
    R44
    1990